MW00477611

SEVYN

THE SMOKE & FIRE SERIES

BESTSELLING AUTHOR
KETA KENDRIC

Keta Kendric

Sevyn: The Smoke & Fire Series

Second Edition

Copyright © 2022 by Keta Kendric

Cover art by Mayhem Cover Creations

Editors: A.L. Barron, K. Alex Walker, & Tam Jernigan.

ISBN: 978-1-956650-01-3

CONTENTS

To the dreamers who give their minds the gift of escaping this reality.

SUMMARY OF THE SMOKE & FIRE SERIES

The Smoke & Fire Series is a slow build into a paranormal world of lovable heroes and diabolical villains. The series' heroes and heroines are tragically flawed and some will straddle the line between good and evil. The characters are forced to learn themselves while discovering undeniable romances. They will embrace abilities that can help them navigate a developing supernatural world as well as survive forces intent on unleashing pure unnatural havoc on the *real* world.

SERIES GLOSSARY

TOP (Top Secret Operations Program) - An above top-secret organization that recruits individuals on the supernatural spectrum to catch, capture, or kill supernatural criminals.

The Breeze – The Breeze is the birthplace of life. The Breeze is also known as The Passage and biggest gateway that leads to The Vault, the second dimension it birthed, and The Hollow, the third dimension it birthed.

The Vault – A place created or born from the Breeze. Individuals from the Vault are called Mist Makers or Smokies and no longer possess a physical body. Their energy signature registers as *life* because the essence of their soul is still intact. They can travel through certain gates and energy fields that other individuals cannot.

The Hollow – A place created or born from the Breeze. Individuals from the Hollow are called Blazers and no longer possess a physical body. Their energy signature registers as *death* because a part of their soul has been sucked into The Hollow. The Hollow is said to be the gateway to hell.

Brazen – Children created from fire and darkness and born in the Hollow.

Gleaner – Individuals recruited in the Hollow to collect and assist souls with their transition into the Hollow. These are blazers who have earned the title of Gleaner.

Huntress – Supernatural female whose sole purpose is to hunt and kill vampires. A huntress' need to kill vampires is said to be three times stronger than a vampire's thirst for blood.

Bendy - Individuals with the ability to cross the lines that connect the past, present, and the future. These individuals possess a unique element that allows them to exist in the multi-dimensional space-time continuum and can encompass the past, present, and future at the same time.

Hyphenated – Supernatural being with multiple abilities.

Toddler – Any supernatural being that is unknowledgeable or untrained in ways of the supernatural. Many believe that they are human.

Hindered – An underdeveloped supernatural being who, for reasons unknown, is delayed from reaching their supernatural maturity.

Vampires, Were animals, Shifters, Witches – All supernatural beings that are assumed myths by *normal* society but have escaped either the Vault or the Hollow and have made the Breeze their home.

Rixie – A spirit, ghost, or phantom with the ability to exist and interact with living beings and matter. Spirits, ghosts, and phantoms are three distinct beings and hate when they are called the wrong name, so referring to them as Rixie is highly suggested.

Bridge – A group of three that are capable of opening a doorway between dimensions. Their purpose is to provide a passageway to souls that may end up in the wrong dimension.

SYNOPSIS

Dana is the pampered daughter of a wealthy diplomat by day, but she hunts monsters at night. After witnessing a brutal home invasion that resulted in her mother's death, she takes extreme measures to avenge her. Tracking the men responsible is arduous work but killing them is next to impossible.

Neal thinks his new assignment, protection for the diplomat's daughter, will be a walk in the park. Trained for combat, the last thing he wants is to babysit some spoiled, rich woman. When he stumbles upon Dana's secret life of monsters and mayhem, he finds he may be the one that needs protecting.

Note: This book is a Re-Release from the version originally published in 2014. Additional action and romance was added to enhance your reading pleasure.

Warning: This book contains violence, explicit language, and sexual content, and is intended for adults. If you don't enjoy paranormal, supernatural, or urban fantasy books, this may not be the book for you.

"Am I the Hero or the Villain?"- Sevyn

CHAPTER ONE

SEVYN

SEVYN WAS LURED from the grips of her slumber by the deep roaring timbre of a male voice. Though she couldn't make out the words, the shrill tone registered desperation, anger even. The shouting continued, assaulting her eardrums. One moment it grew intense and frantic, and the next it was a low hum that faded into the tight grips of drowsiness, waging war on her senses.

Through her sluggish movements, Sevyn managed to shake her head in an attempt to ward off the weariness. She jumped at another loud shout and was introduced to a round of pain in her head that spread like wildfire throughout her body. Her lids fluttered against her roaming eyes, but she didn't have the strength to lift and keep them open.

A new string of shouts sounded, making her temples throb and her eyes squeeze tighter in response to the ache. What was going on?

"Throw down your fucking weapon and exit the vehicle!"

Her head swam, and her focus wavered, but she managed to cling to consciousness. The command was meant for her.

Why are they yelling at me?

1

She pushed aside the heavy ache that made her head lull forward and hang heavy on her shoulders. A throaty groan sounded in response to the urgent call being leveled at her. Determined, she fought fatigue to lift her head. Her body hadn't restored her normal functions, so a weak shake was all she had the energy to offer.

"Throw the weapon down, now! Roll down the window and let me see your hands!"

The demanding words came together like puzzle pieces building a horrific scene, and the worse part was that she was at the epicenter. Had she finally pushed her enemy too hard? There was no doubt in her mind. Her need to avenge her mother's death had placed her here. Right in the hands of the monsters she'd been hunting.

Since the age of fifteen, she'd been on her quest, prodding and poking a hornet's nest in search of the monsters that murdered her mother. No matter how dangerous the hunt, she refused to stop. Her impulse for vengeance had grown into a raging obsession.

Now, here she sat, slumped in the cab of a musty pickup truck with no idea how she'd gotten there. The rearview mirror revealed a shotgun hanging haphazardly behind her head against a cracked, tinted back window.

The barrel of a shiny pistol also appeared in the rearview mirror. Its constant, vibrating movement put a questioning crease in Sevyn's forehead until she grasped that the weapon was in her shivering hand. The crack in the driver's side window was only an inch wide, but it didn't prevent the cold winds of February from sneaking in and finding her.

A threadbare black mechanics jumpsuit, discolored by splatters of paint, dirt, and grime clung loosely to her body. Gas fumes seeped from the material, the thick stench of the fuel making her eyes water and her breaths labored from the burn it left on her lungs.

The nine-millimeter in her hand was aimed at fidgety cops, some pacing with their arms folded across their stiff chests. At least eight surrounded the vehicle. An angry yell for her to drop the weapon came from one who was using a voice amplifier.

Twitchy trigger-fingers caressed the levers of Glocks and nine millimeters aimed at her from every vantage point. The officers located to the east and west of her aimed pump-action shotguns.

Tape and rope kept her immobilized inside the truck, locking her in place along with the weapon she desperately wanted to drop but couldn't. The mildew-tasting rag in her mouth muffled her screams, preventing her from vocalizing her distress to the cops outside. Her mental focus had recovered enough to discern that she was being addressed as *Darrell Wilkins.*

Sevyn was a TOP agent; therefore, it was her job to know the ins and outs of the criminal world. Darrell Wilkins had recently taken credit for killing three cops before dropping off the map.

So, why the hell do they think I'm Darrell Wilkins?

The clues sprouted like weeds in her muddled brain while her situation continued to unfold. Her posed position and the gun taped to her hand was a death sentence. The gag in her mouth stopped her from identifying herself. Her left arm was cuffed to the driver's side door and even her legs were bound. Head and shoulder movements were the only functions that remained.

The culprits who'd staged her had purposely used Wilkins' truck and identity as far as the irate cops knew. Posed for execution, her true identity was obscured by the conditions of her surroundings. The tint in the side windows, her dark clothes, and the overcast Seattle sky showed the officers a darkly shrouded figure aiming a gun at them.

The set-up was well-thought-out. One that left her trapped,

pointing a gun she couldn't put down, at cops who wanted nothing more than revenge. If that wasn't bad enough, Sevyn's firing hand had gone numb and her gas soaked jumpsuit was waiting for a spark.

Her hand, though limp, was suspended, and kept in place by thin rope attached to the ceiling. It was arranged to pull her arm up as an opposing rope tied around the console tugged the same arm in the opposite direction, keeping it in place. The large amount of tape and rope used to secure her to the seat did its job too.

The lighter tint of the windshield allowed her an obscured view of the scene. Her desperate need to speak was blocked by the rag that had soaked up every drop of moisture in her mouth, hindering her ability to spit it out. It was only a matter of time before the yelling outside became flying bullets.

"Humm. Mmm," she groaned uselessly. The shouts outside intensified in volume and repetition, silencing her moans. Even her shivering ceased. Due to loss of circulation, any attempts to move her numb hand would be interpreted as a defensive move and would give the twitchy-fingered cops the green light they needed to pull their triggers.

"Throw down your fucking weapon and exit the vehicle!"

Some barked, one screamed, and a few eagerly divulged that they would blow her brains out. They all agreed on one resounding truth—she needed to drop the weapon.

Sevyn struggled in mind and body. Hunting and underestimating her enemy had landed her in this deadly situation. While hunting monsters, she had shot one of the inhuman bastards in the chest twice, and he'd kept coming. Chest shots usually slowed them down, but not this particular one. He smirked and winked at her before she was struck over the head from behind. The powerful blow had instantly turned her light into darkness.

She'd expected a swift death, a bullet to the head, or a snapped neck, even something as extreme as being dropped from a high-rise. However, her enemy was more creative in the way they wanted to end her life. She was set up to be murdered by police officers who had no idea the world they believed they knew was a dark haven of terror they couldn't even imagine.

Her ability to move faster than the average human had always been her secret advantage. Being able to move faster meant she could anticipate faster; therefore, she wasn't looking forward to seeing death in the form of a bullet coming towards her before it ripped into her body.

The flicker of an unknown object caught her attention. Her gaze shot in the direction of a stand of trees. She studied the area until the outline of a sniper came into focus. He was nearly camouflaged in the dying foliage clinging to a far-off tree. His scope should allow him to see her ropes and tape and he would, hopefully, tell the rest of the group she was being set up. At least, that was what she prayed would happen.

One of the officers advancing on her location shouted once again for her to put the gun down. He stopped directly in front of the truck, peeking over the hood to get a better read on her position.

"Please, put the gun down," he begged. "You don't have to die here today."

Sevyn prayed the sniper's scope would lead him to figuring out her dilemma before his anxious friends fired at her. Given the climate of the world, she was being given a lot of extra leeway where it concerned law enforcement and armed suspects.

A gun blast sounded, the *bang* echoing through the atmosphere and adding a tremble to her thudding heart. The officers scrambled for cover, their wide gapes revealing that they were as surprised as she was by the blast. The cop who'd posted up in front of the truck ducked for cover using the front end to shield himself. Who had fired the shot?

She slouched as low as she could manage, preparing herself

for the firestorm of bullets primed to rip her body to shreds. Tension and fear coursed through her so fiercely, her body shook and caused the cuffs on her left wrist to clink against the unpanelled door. If the bullets didn't kill her, any spark or hot piece of metal would ignite her gasoline-soaked jumpsuit.

The anxious cops maintained their defensive positions, their eyes aimed as steadily as their weapons. Couldn't they tell she wasn't the one shooting?

There was no synchronized call to fire. The blast of guns was the cops' call to action. The first bullet, thankfully, missed its mark, penetrating the body of the truck and not hers. The second, however, flew through the front windshield and whizzed past her face, like a tiny fighter jet.

Shards of glass peppered her face as she struggled against her bindings to avoid sudden death. Shooting pain came alive on the exposed areas of her skin, making her cry out and struggle desperately against her restraints.

Like the projectile of death it was, another bullet headed straight for her head. She yanked her body, forcefully, pulling herself down enough that the bullet narrowly missed her forehead. Having speed in her defensive arsenal had saved her many times, but how many bullets could she dodge before her luck ran out?

Her sharp jerk to avoid the next bullet snapped her gun hand, and she, inadvertently, shot at the cops. The bullet's trajectory exited above the rearview mirror and flew through the windshield. The shot was aimed high enough that it would sail above the determined groups' heads.

Shards of glass dug into Sevyn's face and neck, and she couldn't do anything but duck and blink rapidly to determine which way to move. She cried out, but her muffled moans died before they reached outside the truck.

A bullet ricocheted off the metal of the gun in her hand and shot into her forearm. The searing hot projectile ripped through her arm, releasing echoing waves of pain that forced the numbness away. She stomped her feet, twisted, and turned, but nothing she did freed her from her binds.

Pain was put on hold as she dodged another bullet in the nick of time. The *thump* of bullets pelting the body of the truck kept her twitching and squirming in the seat. In an attempt to duck lower, she stretched her suspended, and now wounded, arm to its limit. The rope dug into her flesh, the rough, hairy threads ripping into her skin. The bullet in her arm burned like acid eating her flesh from the inside out, but she fought the pain to hopefully save her own life.

The driver's side window shattered, bathing her in glass, and another bullet narrowly missed the top of her head. The bullet came so close to killing her, it knocked her wig lopsided. To preserve her identity, she usually wore short-styled wigs when she hunted or worked undercover.

Closing her eyes, she prayed and awaited the final shot that would take her out. She wasn't ready to die, but her immediate horror made her life flash in snapshots inside her head. Her biggest regrets were not seeing her family one last time and not finding and killing the rest of the monsters that had participated in her mother's death.

As abruptly as the shooting had begun, it stopped. Silence pressed down on her, adding weight to the situation while she anticipated the torturous sound of more gunfire. The eerie quiet made the drip-drop of blood flowing from her injured arm sound like the last beats of a dying heart. Had someone finally noticed she was tied to the truck and not an active shooter? Had they noticed that she wasn't Darrell Wilkins?

Sevyn did her best not to squirm as playing dead would help more than attempting to explain her situation. Her head remained slumped forward while she peeked from tearstained eyes. The scrape of a hard-bottomed boot against the pavement grew louder.

"Fuck," the cop grumbled after his first glimpse into the truck.

Another cop in the background yelled, "Hold your fucking fire god-dammit!"

At her window now, the one who approached stood at an angle where Sevyn couldn't turn to see him fully.

"Put the gun down!" he ordered, his breaths rushing in quick spurts. "Let me see both your hands!"

She remained immobile and prayed the cop took a few steps closer to see the full extent of her situation. The sound of his breaths blew from his nose and mouth, and she sensed him assessing her.

"It's a female!" His voice boomed through the busted window. "Someone tied her to the truck. Fuck. Fuck. Fuck!" he shouted with a thunderous roar.

The cop's head, the one who had taken refuge in front of the truck, reappeared. Sevyn peeked through one squinted eye, unsure of how soon to reveal that she was still alive. The man in front of the truck stared, unmoving. She imagined she was a sight, sitting there tied to a truck that had been through its own war.

Confidence rushed in and pushed through her veins, urging her to raise her head and glance at the cop at her window. He gasped and drew back at her movement, his wide-eyed gaze roaming her trussed up body. She lifted her head higher, so he would see the rag in her mouth.

A shaky hand reached out.

"Ma'am, I'm going to remove the rag."

Thank God.

As soon as the rag was removed, she coughed, gagging on the sudden rush of air she sucked in. The flame she must have unknowingly swallowed made her dry, scratchy throat ignite with hacking jerks. The cop leaned into the truck, his eyes jetting around the space and taking in the duct tape, rope, and cuffs keeping her in place.

"Whoever did this, they did a number on you, lady," he mumbled, low and more to himself than her. "Who'd you piss off?"

She struggled, attempting to speak but sound wanted no part of her raw throat. Her ragged voice scraped her vocal cords, but she remained unable to form words to let the cop know her name. Her attention was snatched away from the help at her side when her quick eye landed on something worse than gun-wielding police officers.

The bastard, or one of the sons of bitches who'd arranged this entire setup, stooped in a stand of bushes baring holey leaves and fighting the cold to stay alive. He was far enough away that the cops hadn't noticed him. He'd likely been there the entire time, waiting to bear witness to her death and was no doubt the asshole who'd fired the first shot. The officers were too busy ogling *her* to notice *him*, but she didn't miss his pale face and the evil smile he flashed.

"Next time." His thin lips conveyed his silent pledge.

He knew she would see him because his eyes were as sharp and as quick as hers.

"Ma'am," the cop at her window called, attempting to get her attention, but her eyes remained on the devil in the bushes. His words were a promise that he would kill her the next time they encountered each other.

Since the cops weren't aiming to kill her anymore, an untapped fury sparked within Sevyn and heightened her need to destroy the demon posing as a man. He was bold enough to stand from his stooping position, and before he could turn away, she silently mouthed, *"You're dead."*

The teasing smirk that bent his thin lips confirmed he'd received her message.

Fingers snapped in front of her face along with the cop's commanding voice, drawing her from her silent promise.

"Ma'am, are you okay? Can you speak? What's your name?"

The quick shot of fury that had flooded her system evaporated and allowed her voice to find its way through the rough patches of her throat.

"My name is Dana Diallo. My father is William Diallo."

Her father's name held weight and would guarantee that she'd be treated with more respect.

The cop's jaw dropped, his searching gaze scanning hers for confirmation. "William Diallo, the self-made millionaire, entrepreneur, and diplomat? Get outta here."

I wish I could.

Somewhere in the distance, a cop yelled a late announcement. "Lower your weapons. It's a woman. She's been setup. It's not Wilkins."

The cop peeking in through her window announced he would cut her loose before the truck door squeaked open. Finally, she released the pressure on her injured arm and relished the fact that she wasn't going to die today. She would have another chance to catch her mother's killers. The biggest question on her mind, *Am I going to be the one introducing them to Death or will they be the ones making the introductions?*

CHAPTER TWO

DANA

Dana rarely watched television, but there were a few segments that captured her attention from time to time. Eleanor Garcia was a Hispanic reporter who had a knack for chasing down supernatural stories and capturing images of paranormal sightings.

Thankfully, most of Eleanor's media journalist counterparts assumed she was crazy or maybe using her supernatural work as an angle to keep herself in the spotlight. Due to skepticism and ridicule, Eleanor was loved more for the entertainment value of her work over its validity.

"So...Eleanor," her interviewer, Jake Simmons called out, skepticism dripping off his voice. *"You want the world to believe that there are superhumans roaming the planet and that heaven and hell are real dimensions borne from ours here on earth?"* Jake attempted but failed to keep a smirk off his face. His gaze on the camera plainly showed he didn't believe a word she was saying.

"You don't have to believe me, Jake," she replied, keeping her own gaze aimed at the camera. *"There are more than enough people out there who believe me, many who have encountered the supernatural. And..."*

She stretched out the word *and* for dramatic effect.

"It's not heaven and hell born of this dimension, but two other dimensions called the Vault and the Hollow."

Jake lifted a disbelieving brow and the corner of his lip hiked in response.

Eleanor straightened in her chair, her face settling into a serious expression. *"There are two theories to be considered when you encounter the unexplained, the supernatural, and the myths and legends that have been reduced to nothing more than entertainment."*

Her informative tone indicated that Jake's mocking actions didn't bother her one bit.

"And those theories are?" he questioned before turning his condescending expression back on the camera.

Eleanor focused on the camera. Her next words meant for the people out there who would take them seriously. *"The first is the theory of Intermingling Time. It states that we are one intermingling world, past, present, and future. The past and the future were always in a constant state of war over what events in an individual's life took precedence. The present, a neutral party, remains stuck in the middle of the never-ending battle. When the ongoing feud between the past and future threatened to rip apart the present, a shaky alliance was formed. The problem is no one world can exist without the others."*

Jake lifted one high-arching brow, the smile in his gaze reaching his lips. Eleanor's rants were no doubt boosting the show's ratings.

"The second is the theory of Dimensional Evolution. It proposes this world is made up of three interlocking dimensions. We were originally one dimension, but through the natural process of death, there had to be a place created for our energies, mental and spiritual, to go after it exited our bodies. The Vault and the Hollow were born when the buildup of energy forces started to rip apart the natural structure of this dimension. Within the Vault and the Hollow, your energy force is free to manifest whatever the mind conjures because your body is no longer there to blanket the realities your energy

signature has the capacity to create. The Vault and Hollow are the true gateways for your soul's ascension to Heaven or descension to Hell."

Jake placed a finger under his chin and drew closer to her with tightly squinted eyes. *"Your theories actually sound interesting, but how do you explain the supernatural individuals that are supposed to exist here in this dimension? And, this second theory sounds like something that some deep thinking meditators already believe. Some believe our world is manifested in our minds and reality is no more than an image the mind created. That when we close our eyes, we don't see anything because it never existed in the first place. We're nothing more than energy."*

She appeared pleased, or even intrigued by his questions and statements.

"The answer is simple. Those from the Vault and the Hollow found a way back to this dimension. And..."

Dana had heard enough. She turned the volume down on her television and stepped over to her bedroom window. She secretly hunted supernatural criminals for her agency, TOP, and even she found it difficult to believe in all of Eleanor's claims.

The rain poured in sheets outside, temporarily washing the world of its evil. At least, that was what Danalyn Diallo believed. The sound of rain relaxed her, the sight of it hypnotizing, and the shimmering beauty of it eased her mind. Rain was Dana's therapy, a form of meditation that kept her sane in a world filled with chaos.

From her side of the glass, her fingers traced the beautiful droplets that drizzled down the outside of the windowpane like happy tears. Reluctantly, she turned away from the view to dress and prepare for another boring day.

Her mind went off on a tangent, dredging up memories on how she'd become her alter ego Sevyn. She'd been recruited into the Top Secret Operations Program, TOP, run by the government. Some called it a supernatural police unit, and some labeled it a secret branch of the military dedicated to hunting monsters hell-bent on destroying the world.

The agency had apparently had eyes on her for years. When they pulled her in and produced footage of her making her first kill, she'd assumed she would be facing a life sentence. It had taken her three years to track one of her mother's killers, but at eighteen, she'd been an amateur and her sloppy execution had gotten her caught. TOP was not like any agency she'd heard about or knew of. Instead of punishing her for killing a man in cold blood, they recruited her.

At the time, she had no way of knowing she hadn't actually killed a *person*. Nevertheless, she hadn't needed much convincing to accept the agency's proposal. She was provided years of top notch training, and the day she turned twenty-one, TOP activated her. Due to their training program, her fighting, tracking, and killing skills improved tenfold. Those skills were used to track down suspects for the agency as well as continue her personal quest.

Dana smiled away the thoughts while glancing at herself in the mirror. Beautiful, classy, and smart were words people used to describe her. The words were descriptors that she aimed to make true when presenting herself to family and friends. No one on a personal level knew her as Sevyn, and she would never disclose her secret identity to them for their own protection.

As a TOP asset, her agency had a hand in helping her downplay the truck scene that had gotten her shot in the arm a few months ago. A botched kidnapping attempt was what was released to the public. Every cop involved that day had drafted their reports to match the far-fetched story. Dana didn't know the details of how the agency had convinced those cops to lie, but she was grateful.

The agency employed several types of agents and groups, some who tracked deadly supernatural beings through digital means, and agents like herself, who captured or terminated the monsters to keep them from turning the world into their dumpster.

When her mind began to spiral into the part of her life she believed she had become obsessed with, Dana reminded herself that she was the dutiful daughter now, and not the spy.

Along with her brothers, Daniel and David, they ran the family business, Diallo Investments. Although her father was CEO of the firm, William chose to embrace his job as a diplomat. He specialized in foreign relations between the U.S. and a number of participating nations.

Dana had no clear idea of what specific duties her father's specialty entailed because he never spilled any of his job secrets. She'd assumed what diplomats did for a living until she found out she didn't have a clue. Job secrets and secret jobs was an interesting paradox she shared with her father.

She defied many of the requests and demands thrusted upon her by the Diallo men. Their aim was to get her married and settled into a nice cushy life, but she would never be content with being a stay-at-home prize to a man who didn't deserve her. She played by her own rules when it came to men, and it drove her father and brothers crazy.

She appeased them by acting her part as the dutiful daughter and hardworking younger sister, to a certain point. To keep an eye on her, her father made her a portfolio manager in the family's investment firm. It was a position she'd begrudgingly accepted four years ago after earning her master's degree.

Her passion was never to work for her father, but the job turned out to be a blessing in disguise and provided her a valuable cover. In a way, she and her father were using each other to get what they believed they needed. She needed to find her mother's killers, and her father needed to protect her.

The financial security her family provided was a blessing too, but Dana refused to bask solely in the good life while the real world went to hell in a flaming hand basket. The real world operated under veils of evil so insidious, it would make heads spin—literally. She didn't want to become soft and unaware, so she refused to remain sheltered under her family's financial umbrella and hired security.

She was more inclined to find ways to make the world safer by tracking down one supernatural killer at a time versus picking out China, choosing flower arrangements, or attending teas and balls among the clueless. Her mother, Natalya Diallo, had been the consummate mother and socialite. When Dana was younger, she'd been groomed to follow in her mother's footsteps.

Despite the comforts and security in her family's life, her mother had died during a horrific home invasion that left the entire family gutted. Her mind shattered the night she witnessed her mother's death.

The crime had done irreparable damage to her young psyche, leaving her ranting about monsters eating her mother's flesh. The nightmare had led her to sleepwalking and screaming the walls down some nights. Her outbursts and actions eventually landed her in the offices of countless shrinks. The fact that no wounds had been found on her mother's body led her family to believe that Dana had truly suffered a psychotic break after witnessing the death.

Her father, as much as he fought to hide it, had never gotten over his wife's death either. She witnessed the way he often got lost in thought, and the way sadness covered his face like a mask when he assumed she wasn't paying attention. He blamed himself, saying he hadn't done enough to keep them protected.

Dana stepped away from following in her mother's privileged footsteps and no longer shied away from the harsh realities in life that most wealthy people ignored. Her hunger to seek out and kill the *men* who killed her mother was and would remain her ultimate goal until it was done.

After her mother's death, her father sheltered her and kept

her under protective eyes, so ditching a protection detail became a sport. He was convinced that hired protection was the key to keeping them, namely her, safe. As a result, he had one rule; she could do as she pleased as long as she allowed him to protect her. Her father had relaxed the protection rule drastically, until her latest incident ended with her being trapped in a police standoff and shot in the arm.

Dana glanced up in time to meet the eyes of one of their maids.

"Miss Diallo, your father would like to see you in the study."

"Okay, I'll be down. Thanks."

It was time to meet the newest *victim* her father had hired to babysit her. Without even giving the poor man a chance, she was already formulating in her head ways to get rid of him. She didn't need or want protection. Protection got in her way when it was time for her to hunt.

CHAPTER THREE

NEAL

Neal Erickson trailed his fingers through his dirty blonde hair and let his green eyes fall to the digital profile on his phone that highlighted the elements of his next assignment. He'd been an agent for TOP for five years and didn't understand why he was being assigned a job babysitting the daughter of a wealthy diplomat.

He was not one to boast about his abilities, but he usually received more serious jobs, like tracking murderers or taking down rogue combatants. His jobs usually involved murders in cases that defied logic and science, or individuals whose genetic makeup was outside of what the world considered normal.

He didn't know whether he should be upset about the job downgrade or relieved as it could serve as a respite from his otherwise hard work. Trained for combat, the last thing he wanted was to babysit some spoiled, rich woman. However, he prided himself on not being a complainer. He'd accepted the assignment and kept his comments on the matter to himself.

If there was one thing Neal had learned in his line of work, it was that nothing was ever as it seemed. The file he received from the agency on Danalyn Diallo detailed a story that had him questioning how she had ended up in a situation that led to her being shot by cops. Since his agency had taken the case, it meant she or her family had encountered, was the target of, or was about to face something they weren't going to be able to explain logically. Despite his questions, Neal approached his new assignment determined to keep an open mind.

The family home where he would be staying for the duration sat about ten miles from the nearest neighbor on a carefully picked plot of land at the foot of the Olympic mountains. Here, the evergreen forests accepted kisses from lakes, and the bodies of waters reached out and hugged the curves of the mountains.

The views alone were enough to make him pull over twice and admire them, despite the indecisive temperament of the rain. The scenery was alive with insects and animals crooning and harmonizing together. The trees were inspired by light brushes of wind to whisper their own sweet melodies, and the water added its lyrical flow that poured perfection into the landscape.

Neal had been in Seattle for three days now, and although the rain rested periodically, it never lost its eagerness to show off its flowing patterns of wet beauty. This must have been the city that coined the saying, "April showers bring May flowers" because the April rains were readying the blooms. He noticed, while in the city, most of the people didn't mind the rain, but he would have to acclimate to it.

He was greeted at the front gate of the well-appointed Diallo estate by an armed guard who conducted himself with military exactness. The guard, with his wide brown eyes, stocky build, and dark hair checked his paperwork and ID and then proceeded to examine his rented, black Dodge Charger with a sophisticated scanner that belonged at the entrance to the White House instead of a private residence.

The guard opened the large wrought iron outer gates of the property and pointed Neal to a secondary entrance that led to a massively guarded gray and white stone mansion. Neal was greeted by a second armed guard waiting in the driveway with a large black umbrella.

"Hello. Name's Howard."

"Nice to meet you. I'm Neal," he introduced himself, reaching for the guard's offered hand. Howard was tall and fit and resembled a member of SWAT more than a member of a personal protective detail. The combat boots, dark blue cargo pants, and long sleeved button ups appeared to be the standard for this crew. The only thing missing was riot gear.

Neal shook water from his collar but turned down the umbrella Howard offered. When the man marched up the steps to the entranceway that opened to a barred walkway and two large metal doors, he followed without a word. Howard used a key card and then a numeric code to gain access into the house.

Once he stepped inside, Neal noticed more guards posted at discreet locations within the house, some standing so still they blended into the background. The diplomat was serious about protecting his family and had this place fortified and guarded like a prison. Did they already know about the secrets this world kept?

The house appeared larger inside than it had from the outside. It exuded a high level of sophistication and class, displaying beautifully crafted French-style furnishings with modern allure. Areas on the walls where pictures normally hung had original handcrafted and carved art etched directly into the wall itself. There were life-size statues and vases that put museum showpieces to shame.

The Diallos were loaded. The diplomat's salary was pennies compared to what he actually made as a successful entrepreneur. Being a diplomat, however, garnered a certain level of power that most successful people thrived on. Despite what the public believed they knew; diplomatic immunity had many definitions and was one of the best perks of the job.

Neal was escorted to a large study. The size and well-stocked bookshelves made the space resemble the lobby of an exclusive library. He didn't miss the curious smile resting on Howard's lips while he suggested Neal take a seat. Based on the gleeful glint in his eyes and the energetic buzz pouring off his body, Howard was itching to leak information Neal wasn't sure he wanted to hear. It was too soon to start hearing and dissecting rumors. When he didn't comment on the man's waiting smile, Howard started a conversation anyway.

"If you're here for the daughter, good luck, buddy," he teased. "She is a handful. When she's not charming her way into getting what she wants, she uses her cleverness to trick her way into getting what she wants."

Neal offered Howard a weakly lifted brow as a reply.

"I must warn you, one of her most lethal weapons is her beauty. The woman should be labeled, 'against the law.' She doesn't flaunt her looks, but it's difficult not to notice. If she wanted to, she could use it as a superpower. Let me also warn you ahead of time, everyone her father has hired in the last few years for her personal protection detail has ended up quitting or requesting a transfer."

Neal didn't comment, but the statement made his brow lift higher. Howard's foot tapped rapidly to contain his need to spill more gossip. "Mr. Diallo knows his daughter is no angel, but no one had better not say otherwise."

Howard stepped off but spun on his heels with a hand lifted to drive home whatever else he was preparing to say.

"Oh. I almost forgot. Although she'll disrupt your efforts to protect her, keep in mind that there is a threat lurking. She downplayed being shot in the arm, but there may be someone trying to kill her. She's had numerous brushes with death in the past four years and every incident is followed up with dead end leads. She was also an eyewitness to her mother's murder when she was a little girl, and the killers were never found. It's one of the reasons Mr. Diallo keeps so many guards in place."

Neal gave a nod, and although he knew the information, he took heed of Howard's warnings. He had already studied the diplomat, his three children, and the latest incident that had gotten the daughter shot. Although he had yet to figure out why, this woman he'd never met face to face had sparked his interest.

Neal jumped to his feet at the sound of William Diallo's approaching footsteps. William entered the room with a ready smile. After taking Neal's offered hand, he held it with a firm grip, flexing his strength. His body hummed with a warm, welcoming energy that coaxed a smile onto Neal's lips.

"Son, I already like you. You know how to show a man respect."

Neal inclined his head, unsure if it was a statement or compliment. William released his hand and gestured with a nod for Neal to take a seat.

"Is it okay if I call you Neal? Calling you Mr. Erickson is a little too formal for me."

"Yes. Neal is fine."

Neal noticed the man's distinct accent and remembered reading he was originally from Nigeria.

William approached the tray of refreshments one of the maids had set out and poured himself a drink. He carried out his action the way he carried himself, with grace and ease.

He glanced over his shoulder at Neal. "Would you like a drink?"

"I never drink on the job."

A proud smile inched across William's mouth.

"Good. I need you with a clear head if you're to keep my daughter safe."

The man kept a keen eye on him while taking his seat.

"I need to explain a few things to you about my daughter." William took a long sip of his drink. "I'm no fool when it comes to her. Dana's polite and proper in front of me and guests, but I know better. My daughter is strong-willed and determined, and although she hides it from me, I know she's usually up to something she doesn't want me or her brothers to know about. I have never snooped into her private business, but that doesn't mean I won't do everything in my power to ensure her safety."

Another sip emptied his glass.

"She's a complex one for sure. Hardheaded and, at the same time, sweeter than sugar cubes. Dana doesn't listen or take orders well and is used to getting her way or finding a way to get her way. I can't say she's spoiled, but she does like to live well. The girl knows how to downplay her intellect. She'll have you thinking she's clueless when she knows the answer all along."

William paused smiling and aiming his gaze at the wall ahead of him, musing on some thought swirling in his head. "She gives me ulcers, but I love her to death and will do anything to protect her. But I'll be damned if trying to protect her isn't one of the most difficult tasks I've undertaken."

William cared deeply for his daughter. It was embedded in the creases of his face, in the tilt of his smile when he spoke of her, and in the flash of his eyes when he thought about her.

"Neal, you have come highly recommended from a good friend of mine, and I'm counting on you to keep my girl safe, by any means."

How much trouble could one woman be?

Pushing the button on a remote, William spoke into the device, asking one of his maids to track down his daughter and have her meet him in the study.

Neal had no idea why he was anxious about meeting this woman who had a reputation for being a bit of a troublemaker.

He was a well-trained agent, measured among the deadliest and most well-equipped mercenaries in the country.

Why am I anxious?

He knew from the file he'd received on the diplomat that William Diallo was in his late fifties, but the man didn't look a day over forty. His skin was as dark as midnight, which made his smile stand out and his dark eyes shimmer.

He'd had two sons with his first wife who'd died of cancer and had later re-married. Dana was a product of his second marriage. William's voice drew Neal's attention.

"As you can see, Dana likes to keep her old man waiting."

William stood and poured himself a second drink before retaking his seat. Neal's gaze landed on the man's fingers drumming on the glass-topped table next to him. He glanced up occasionally and flashed a subtle smile like words were escaping him.

The click-clack of heels traveling down the hall signaled the daughter's approach and stole Neal's attention from William's peculiar behavior.

When Dana stepped through the door, Neal's gaze started at her feet and didn't stop until it rested on her face. Years of practice in keeping a poker face helped conceal his surprise. The guard, Howard, had been right. The diplomat's daughter was stunning.

Her beauty was evident, but she possessed an extra layer of smooth confidence that amplified it enough to take his breath and keep it before deciding to let him breathe again. Discipline be damned, she had an aura about her that made him stare. She was poised yet relaxed, imposing yet welcoming, classy yet sexy. The woman was a walking contradiction of the most impressive features he'd ever seen.

Her face was an uncommonly beautiful mix of fresh and fine, her features soft and delicate. Neal lost his poker face again, watching. Her complexion was a creamy brown or deep caramel depending on the angle in which the light bounced off her skin. She was lighter than her father, but their features, especially the eyes and nose, bore a likeness that unquestionably made William her father.

Her skin was perfectly hued, like an artist had mixed different shades of brown until the mixture breathed perfection. She wore light but noticeable makeup that made her big brown eyes pop, and her shimmering lip gloss highlighted full, lush lips. Incredibly long lashes, he noticed at a distance, sat under perfectly arched brows. And they were her real lashes, not those big sets of bushes women were stapling to the tops of their eyes lately.

Her navy-blue skirt suit was so exquisitely constructed; it appeared the designer himself had paid her a casual visit. The skirt kissed well-defined legs that supported a frame sporting sassy curves. The deep V cut of the jacket gave way to a sheer tan top beneath.

Thankfully, her preoccupation with her father kept her from noticing him checking out her attention-getting figure. Her sexy, tan ankle boots added flavor, but should have been illegal throughout the country. He had never seen heels that high. If he had to guess, she was probably five-six, seven at the most, but the heels made her appear closer to six feet.

In the few seconds it had taken her to walk into the room, he had committed her to memory. Her presence was enough to throw him off-kilter, and it didn't help that her perfume added to the grip she had on his senses. The beautiful scents of spice viburnum and peony were sweet and persuasive like her contradictive appearance. The fragrance acted as a prelude to the woman he would soon face.

Her arm was looped around her father's. Her tone remained low as she shared a comment with him that made him laugh out loud. Neal had already determined that he would be on constant guard with her. He hadn't even uttered a word to her, yet he felt like they'd had a conversation.

Dana placed a delicate peck on her father's cheek and took her time wiping her lip gloss from his face. William waited until she was done before taking her by a perfectly manicured hand and turning her to face Neal.

"Dana, I'd like to introduce you to Mr. Neal Erickson. He's going to look after you until things are safe for us again. Sweetheart, I want you to treat Mr. Erickson with the utmost respect."

He addressed her as a father would an unruly child with a twinge of discipline in his tone. Her lips pursed before she released a long-winded sigh.

"Dad…honestly, when is our family ever going to be safe? I have no intention of spending the rest of my days being watched and followed."

William gave her the *please-don't-scare-this-poor-guy-away* stare before his gaze shuffled between her and Neal.

A few careful steps drew her closer while she observed him for the first time. At first, she appeared poised to unleash her attitude, but her posture softened, and she reached out her hand.

"Mr. Erickson, nice to meet you."

"Miss Diallo, nice to meet you as well," Neal stated, taking her hand.

The fact that she targeted his eyes and not the distinct scar that spanned a portion of his right eye and traveled along his cheek spoke volumes about her personality. He was used to people zeroing in on his scar like it was the sum of him. Dana did the opposite, which was an impressive feat, considering his scar was a hard target to miss. He searched her eyes for truth or deception and found only a hint of mischief reflected back at him. She was dangerous. He sensed it in the firmness of her prolonged handshake.

Was she sizing him up or checking him out? He couldn't tell.

She came across as delicate, pampered, and wealthy, but he sensed that she was showing him exactly what she wanted him to see. He realized, a few seconds too late, that no other person had the ability to sway him this easily. Within seconds, she had found a way in and made him lose focus.

Once she'd let him stare long enough, she loosened her grip on his hand and turned away, returning her attention to her father. Neal reclaimed his game face, or, at least, tried. It was wise to remember that Dana had the ability to pull attention from her father and most likely every man she encountered.

Don't fall for it.

A glance was cast over her shoulder at Neal like she was tuned into his thoughts. "It's nice meeting you, Mr. Erickson."

"You as well Miss Diallo," he replied, fighting to keep his eyes from sweeping her body one last time.

Her father took a hold of her hand to stop her from walking away.

"Honey, wait. Are you going out today? I'd like Neal to escort you."

Although it was a fake one, she flashed her father a smile that still managed to outshine the lights in the vaulted ceiling.

"I'm going to relax in my room, so you don't have to stress about me going anywhere and getting my head blown off my shoulders." She pointed one of those perfect French-tipped nails in Neal's direction. "You can send Mr. Erickson to my room if that will ease your mind. You worry too much."

The stress lines that stretched across William's forehead deepened. "Honey, you know I don't like you talking about getting killed. I'll see you for dinner later."

He kissed her forehead before letting her proceed out of the room.

"See what I have to deal with, Neal? My boys are so easy. Having a daughter is delicate and stressful work. But I don't know what I'd do if something happened to my baby girl."

Neal could almost touch the care in William's voice. Although he didn't have children and never considered having any of his own, he was fairly certain he understood the father's concerns.

William lifted a hand, his finger stiff in a way that hinted at a warning. "I want you to take the room across the hall from Dana's and, whatever you do, do not underestimate my daughter's ability to do whatever she wants, no matter *who* is protecting her."

William paused and Neal could see him thinking.

"My sons, Daniel and David, will be here later this evening. You'll get a chance to meet them, then."

Neal nodded, but observed William intently, heeding another warning from the worried father about his daughter. For the second time that day, the question crossed his mind, *Can one woman be that much trouble?*

He told himself his attraction to Dana was nothing more than his dry spell wreaking havoc on his senses. A series of back-to-back assignments hadn't allowed him any downtime. As a result, he hadn't been with a woman, let alone touched one, in months. A woman like Dana wouldn't give him a second glance anyway, so there was no use wasting time thinking about her.

CHAPTER FOUR

NEAL

LATER THAT EVENING, Neal met the Diallo brothers at what the family called a small dinner party. A small party for them accommodated at least fifty guests who mingled about the family's oversized dining room. Food was served from three tables, each with attendants standing behind trays of steaming platters. A pianist sat behind a beautifully polished grand piano, playing upbeat musical tunes.

Neal was underdressed, in his usual jeans, a plain white T-shirt, and boots but didn't stress about his attire because he was there to protect, not impress. After mingling, he stepped away from the Diallo brothers, David, and Daniel, who'd both voiced their concerns to him about their sister's well-being. Informing him of how she'd forgo spending time with her friends to sneak off to places she didn't want anyone knowing about, or how she often put her life in jeopardy by dodging the security detail.

Everyone in her family was convinced that Dana needed protection except her, and Neal wasn't sure if the family was protecting her from an unknown enemy or herself. Was he missing something? Was the Diallo family not disclosing something to him about Dana that he needed to know?

He kept an eye on her, observing how she played her role, acting innocent and docile in front of her family, but he wasn't fooled. Every instinct he possessed screamed that she was anything but what she conveyed to her family. He hadn't had any alone time with her but based on the side notes he had gotten from her family and the guard, he would venture to say she was definitely putting on a good performance.

She had changed into a white, silk jumpsuit that likely cost more than he made in a month. Like her earlier attire, the suit appeared to have been sewn onto her body, hugging her curves, and gliding along her tempting frame.

In the blink of an eye, he lost sight of her which left him searching for where she could have gone. He turned in a slow, scanning circle and surmised she must have ducked out of the room.

"You're in deep thought, Mr. Erickson. Are you thinking about me?"

His head jetted around, surprised that she'd sneaked up on him. "Call me Neal. And yes, I was thinking about you."

Her brows lifted in surprise at his straightforward answer, and he enjoyed seeing the expression on her face. He got the sense that she wasn't easily stunned.

"I was thinking about how good a performance you're putting on in front of your family. Thankfully, I can see deeper than your surface."

One of those perfectly arched brows lifted high on her forehead.

"Everyone is entitled to their opinions, Mr. Erickson. And even if you can see deeper, like you seem to think, you couldn't handle what's under my surface."

This time, his eyebrows shot up. She had purposely ignored his request to address him as Neal, and her words were as sharp as ten-thousand tacks.

"My opinion is right, *Miss Diallo*. And I'm sure I wouldn't have a problem handling what's under your surface."

He enjoyed a glimpse at another priceless crease of surprise his statement left on her face. He had trouble deciding if they were flirting or waging war. She closed the space between them so quickly, the action left him unable to stop the quick knot of recoiling tension that made his body hitch.

Another pair of those illegal heels were on her feet and helped to set her eyes inches below his six-two frame. Peering up at him, her gaze projected a daring glint that captured his sensible resolve.

"Save yourself the trouble, Mr. Erickson. I would devour you."

He'd never been one to back down from a fight, or whatever it was they were doing, so he met her thunderous gaze with a glint just as strong. At this point, they were so close to each other the warm flow of her breath stroked his face.

"Miss Diallo, you have obviously never been disciplined. The only way you will devour me is if I let you."

One of those lovely eyebrows lifted a hair before a smile danced across her eyes but never touched her lips.

"We'll see," were the last words she declared before giving him back his personal space. She turned to face the party, her side view showing him her territorial stance. He breathed in a slow but deep breath.

What the hell just happened?

He'd never had a word-sparring contest with anyone like that before. This was their first conversation, but it didn't stop them from bantering back and forth like they were already acquainted.

Dana shot him one last daring glance before walking away.

Neal forced himself, once again, to concentrate on the reason he was there in the first place—to protect her. She was putting on a performance, but what she didn't know was that he could put one on as well. He had no doubt they would clash like two titans, but the craziest thing about the situation was, he believed he would enjoy the battle.

DANA

The next morning.

The creases of a devious smile bent the corners of her red painted lips. Dana was up to no good and would have thought less of herself if she didn't attempt to get one over on her new babysitter. Last night, he had surprised her. No one other than her father and brothers called her out or took a stance against her, but she had to admit she enjoyed Neal's challenge.

Nevertheless, it appeared ditching her new sitter would be easier than she assumed considering how highly her father said he'd come recommended. Unlike her last three or four protectors, Neal was more relaxed. He didn't hover or watch her like a hawk, nor did he appear the least bit impressed with her. The notion vexed her a little. Her appearance had gotten her through many situations and so had her speed, and she wasn't sorry for using whatever she had in her arsenal to accomplish her missions.

Smiling, she reflected on her brief interactions with Neal. Plainly dressed in jeans and a fitted long-sleeved T-shirt, he was attractive. Her up close view allowed her to see that he was toned in all the right places and possessed a pair of mesmerizing blue-green eyes that captured her attention at the slightest glance. His dirty blond hair complemented lightly tanned skin and well-defined, kissable lips.

Thinking of his lips, she found herself wanting to trace the lines of them with her tongue. His height was also a contender for her attention, standing taller than a well-designed skyscraper. A first for her, she found herself immediately attracted to Neal.

"Don't go there, Dana," she reminded herself with a low murmur.

He might fool her father, but she knew better. She sensed that Neal had secrets. Lots of them. Dana shook off thoughts of her hot new babysitter and returned to her devious task at hand.

At five in the morning, Neal was in bed, and she was making a clean getaway by leaving two hours earlier than she had informed him. She hummed the tune to *Jeopardy!* while the garage door rose. A glimpse of the red and orange hues of the horizon stretching above the trees drew her attention. The daylight was still whispering the darkness away, charming it into leaving behind a beautiful dim glow.

She navigated the car down the driveway, while the gate slinked open at a lingering pace. Two of the guards waved, unable to see inside her black Mercedes S580 due to its dark tint. Neither man stopped her to make sure Neal was with her, assuming he automatically would be.

She turned onto the road that would lead her to the little slice of privacy she sought. Finally alone, she relished the hour long drive ahead of her, the ferry she'd have to catch, and even the traffic she'd have to fight in the city. The sight of the gate closing in her rearview mirror put a smile on her face, and she breathed in the liberating sense of relief swirling inside.

"I'm free," she giggled, proud of her early morning actions.

"What are you free of, Miss Diallo?"

The voice leaped across her seat and struck her in the back of the head before landing in her ears. She jerked the steering wheel, nearly sending the car into one of the two-hundred-year-old trees that lined their isolated street.

Neal's sudden appearance sent her heart into a thundering rush of erratic beats before it climbed out of her chest and landed on the passenger seat. He sat in her backseat, eyeing her in the rearview mirror. Though her lips were parted and her eyes wide, she couldn't spit out any words, not even if someone else spoke them for her.

"What?" How the hell had he gotten back there? "You...you."

The twisted little smirk on his face hinted that he'd enjoyed scaring her half to death. When she initially climbed into her car, she was certain he hadn't been in the vehicle. Or had he been? His gaze continued to mock her in the mirror.

"Miss Diallo, my job is to protect you, not lie in bed asleep while you make attempts to sneak away. I had a sneaking suspicion you would try something."

She cleared her throat, her irritation and curiosity fighting for dominance. "Call me Dana. And yes, I thought you were asleep. There's only one thing I want and that is alone time. You don't know how it feels to be under the watchful eye of someone every waking moment of every day."

He sat up higher in the back seat, giving her a clearer view of his face in the mirror. "Miss Diallo, I understand your situation better than you might think, but I wouldn't be here if you didn't have a legitimate threat on your life. You may not like it, but until we eliminate the threat, you're stuck with me."

Her eyes crinkled in frustration. "Mr. Erickson, what makes you think you're going to last that long?"

Even in the mirror, she noted the challenge lingering behind his gaze.

"Call me Neal. And you might be surprised at how crafty, and persistent, I can be. What I lack in looks, I make up for in charisma and cleverness."

He wasn't a pushover; that was for sure. The fact that she liked that about him had her twisting her lips to banish a telling smile, one that had pushed through her frustration. She'd never tell him so, but he was right. He wore charisma and cleverness with confidence. Despite how he viewed himself in the looks department, she was attracted.

She had gotten close enough last night to classify his eyes as either green or blue. His distinct scent was a mix of spicy amber and sandalwood that she should have picked up on the moment she'd jumped into her car. Her eyes had lingered on his lips, which appeared to hold as many secrets as those eyes of his.

Men with facial scars usually wore their hair longer, but not Neal. He wasn't afraid to let you see every part and didn't care if people accepted him or not. He was nothing like the other guards and the first to leave her thinking about him after the briefest introduction.

His scanning eyes in the rearview mirror drew her attention.

"Miss Diallo. Where are you headed? This is not the way to your office."

His voice had grown softer as he glanced around, scanning their surroundings. Despite his shift in tone, it didn't stop her from blowing out an irritated breath.

"Mr. Erickson, like I said before, please call me Dana. And, if you must know, I'd planned to use my freedom doing something I would enjoy, not that you care about my enjoyment."

He released a low grin that plucked at her irritation.

She snatched the steering wheel, sharply making a U-turn. Neal's face dissolved into a frown, along with the words he was about to speak because his body went halfway across the backseat. He gripped the passenger side rear door panel to keep himself upright.

After he straightened, his eyes bore into hers, and the straining level of authoritative intent in them shined through. The rearview mirror was their dividing line.

"Miss Diallo. I didn't say you had to forgo time you would enjoy. I have to stick around, so I can do my job."

The sharpness of her voice intensified. "It's Dana, Mr. Erickson. Call me Dana. My personal enjoyment is just that. Personal.

It won't be the same with company shadowing my every step. I'm better off going to work and making myself productive if I'm going to be watched."

"Neal, call me Neal, Miss Diallo," he said, his voice inching up a notch and the heavy tone tickling her insides despite her irritation. She hid a smirk, knowing she was pissing him off. Was she finally seeing a crack in that handsome poker face of his?

"Maybe we can figure out a way for you to get some personal enjoyment out of your time. I'll keep my distance so you can have a little privacy if that's what you need."

Surprised by this compromise, she didn't answer but appreciated his willingness to make an effort. The smile she was fighting to keep off her face was doing an excellent job of softening her irritation.

CHAPTER FIVE

NEAL

ONCE AT HER OFFICE, Neal scanned every corner of the large, sparsely furnished but immaculately decorated space. A large cherry wood desk sat in the center in front of an executive black leather chair. An array of futuristic metal tables and statues sat in strategic areas and presented a common theme throughout her office.

The place would have been too dim if not for the wall of windows making up one side of the room. The windows were tinted, causing the light to project a hazy glow. The wall to the left was made of floor to ceiling shelves, some housing books and others holding decorative vases and more of those futuristic metal statuettes. Two designer gold-and-red striped chairs sat in front of Dana's desk, which helped to bring color into the space.

A large painting appeared to hover on the wall behind her desk. It was an explosion of colors and, although simple, it was likely as expensive as everything else in the office. Another smaller desk sat displaced near the windows. Neal assumed it was where Dana's former guards had sat, and the sight made him decide to sit elsewhere. The last thing he wanted was to sit so close with her distractingly tempting presence filling his vision and headspace.

Once he was satisfied, and somewhat familiar with her workspace, he planted himself in the entryway, near the exit. The partially mirrored partition built into the front wall gave him an obscured view of her.

He'd picked up on genuine hurt in her tone when she spoke of alone time. Therefore, he wanted to provide her a semblance of privacy. He couldn't imagine going through life under someone's constant guard.

He situated himself so that she wouldn't see him unless she stepped away from her desk.

Occasionally, he glanced up and observed her working, intrigued to find that for a wealthy woman, she didn't mind hard work. She may have had a problem with being told what to do, but she didn't act as spoiled and as privileged as he'd expected.

After a long, silent moment, Neal snapped his head up from his phone.

It's too quiet.

The shuffle of papers and the click of fingers striking the keyboard had stopped. Even the periodic phone conversations had ceased. He'd thought nothing of her bathroom break announcement, but it should have triggered an alarm that she might try something. She couldn't possibly get away through her small bathroom window. It was a twenty-five-story drop.

Neal decided to check on her anyway, figuring he'd better take heed to the repeated warnings about her crafty nature. For all he knew, she already had an escape plan in place.

His first few knocks went unanswered, so he rapped his knuckles harder against the wood. "Miss Diallo, are you okay?"

No answer.

He turned the knob, finding the door locked. She'd been in

there at least ten minutes, enough time for her to formulate a plan.

"Miss Diallo, I'm only going to knock a few more times before I kick this door in."

A muffled *thump* increased his concern.

"Miss Diallo, are you okay? Open the door or I will."

"Give me a second, please," she called, in a tone too pleasant for her.

There was no doubt, she was up to something, but hearing her voice eased a little of his stress. Her beautiful eyes scanned him through the small crack she put in the door before she sprang it the rest of the way open.

She stepped out, her chin tilted up in defiance and her roguish gaze locked with his. A few strands of her hair had fallen from the perfectly pinned bun she favored. She stepped in front of him, taking him in slowly. The amount of mischief pouring from those eyes could have filled an ocean.

"You don't have to wonder what I'm doing every minute of every hour."

A piece of material was thrusted in his direction.

Panties.

The silky piece of material dangled from her finger, dripping wet.

"I had a little accident. Mixed up the dates of my period and had to wash these in the sink." The wet panties were shoved into his hand. "There you have it, proof that I was washing up and not escaping."

Neal didn't believe her one bit and was certain she knew it.

He stood in place, holding a pair of wet blue silk panties. Instead of being shocked by her actions, he checked out her ass when she walked away. Was she wearing any panties now that he was holding the pair she had *supposedly* taken off?

She was up to something, and he wanted to know what.

He cleared his throat. "Miss Diallo, I'm not here to make your life difficult. I'm here in case you need me."

She sat behind her desk and glanced his way. "For the hundredth time, call me Dana."

He kept calling her Miss Diallo because she refused to call him Neal.

He moseyed over to his area and hung her wet panties on the arm of his chair. His job might end up being more difficult than he had anticipated based on the set determination that never seemed to leave Dana's body.

Escape plans and wet panties were just the beginning. She wasn't done by a long shot.

CHAPTER SIX

DANA

Two weeks of following the straight and narrow with Neal, Dana found herself on the verge of going crazy. The day-to-day repetitiveness of it all. She needed the excitement her double life offered, and her father was blocking her with his security geeks.

She was itching to unleash Sevyn, needing to hunt something, or someone.

"You don't talk enough, Mr. Erickson." She took a glimpse of Neal in the passenger seat. "You should talk more."

His gaze didn't meet hers, but she still managed to feel the energy of the attention he focused on her.

"Not much to talk about. I'm your protection. There's no need to get chatty."

She laughed. "If someone wants me dead, or injured, I will be, no matter who's around. The scariest people never reveal how scary they truly are. They *show* you right before they take your life."

Neal tilted his head at her statement, eyeing her with keen intensity like he was attempting to dissect her words. "Point taken, Miss Diallo, but I'm here either way, and I'll do everything in my power to keep you safe."

She studied him as best she could while keeping one eye on the road. There wasn't another man who had the ability to send her curiosity soaring like Neal. Not only was he not like the other guards, but he also wasn't like anyone Dana had ever met. He was calm and relaxed, but he wasn't gullible and damn sure wasn't afraid to speak his mind when he did speak.

His presence held power, pulling her attention even when she fought to ignore him. He possessed several distracting qualities. His strong, solid build and his quiet confidence were a few. There was also the scar on his face that sat above his right eye and made a few sharp turns like a lightning strike along his cheek.

How had he gotten that scar? Despite her aching need to know, she didn't ask. His imperfection made him more interesting, the scar resembling art. It made his face unique in a way she appreciated. No one else would look like him, nor would they ever be able to copy him.

His hodgepodge of incredibly charming features took a hold of her interest and kept a firm grip on it, so tight she was unable to shake it loose. His unapologetic nature along with the quiet strength of his masculinity whispered messages to her femininity, a silent calling unlike any she'd ever experienced.

Neal was sun-kissed, reminding her of the cream and honey she enjoyed in her coffee. He had a low-key charisma that likely melted hearts no matter where he went, and what she found most attractive was that he was unaware of it.

Parked now, she sat in the car staring at him while his gaze bore into hers, casting an expression she couldn't interpret.

"If only I could read thoughts, Miss Diallo."

Her cheeky smile escaped the serious expression she fought to maintain. "My thoughts would probably scare you. They would definitely confuse you. And why do you insist on calling me Miss Diallo? I don't like it. Sounds like you're addressing an elder."

He shrugged. "I keep calling you Miss Diallo for the same reason you keep calling me Mr. Erickson. In reference to your thoughts, I'm sure they would confuse me, but I've been known to catch on quickly and I don't scare easily. You have a cloak of mystery surrounding you, but it won't stop me from doing my job."

She didn't reply. His banter with her should have made her angry, but all it did was add to the reasons she was attracted to him.

NEAL

For the first time, Neal noticed Dana examining his scar. Instead of distaste, interest oozed from her pores. She was one of the few people who saw *him*. Her eyes would meet his every time they were face to face. He hadn't missed the way she studied his mouth when he spoke. Each time their eyes met, he found himself trapped under a sorceress's spell, a weakness he hated to admit.

On the way up to her office, he followed her clicking heels and the view of her delicious ass into a packed elevator. She likely assumed he would let it go and take the next elevator, which would give her time to disappear on him.

He entered the elevator and squeezed past her to the back wall. More bodies piled into the cramped space with every stop, and Dana ended up pressed against him several times. The third time her body collided with his, she didn't back away. Her eyes searched his while her arms remained pinned against his chest. Her probing interest stole his words and left him unable to move the hand he had resting on her waist.

With a stare sharp enough to slice through bone, she dared him to step away until she found the answers she sought. She wanted to know if he was attracted to her, and he'd be damned if he didn't give her the answer when he attempted to remove his hand from her warm body only to have it slide up her arm then back down to her waist.

Finally, she blinked and he was released. Was she using magic? He hadn't picked up the unique energy signature he normally sensed when he interacted with other supernatural individuals.

He stepped away, breaking contact so he could catch his breath. She knew what she was doing to him, and Neal was finding he didn't have any defenses against her.

The man who entered at the next stop would surely breach the elevator's weight limit and send them all plummeting to their deaths. Neal assessed the man who was easily three hundred and fifty pounds. His face was naturally cheerful, the kind of big guy who was skinny at heart.

The man squeezed his large body right next to Dana's, pinning her against Neal whose hands automatically went back to her waist. Her closeness shot waves of longing into him, making his fingers tingle, while her perfume stimulated his senses and had him fighting to keep his eyes from closing.

The last thing he wanted to do was back off, but he couldn't allow her to sense his inability to resist her allure. He dropped his hands and backed away before he became a puddle under the crowd's feet.

Once they left the elevator and entered her office, he returned to his post while she worked. After spending hours sitting, she periodically paced behind her desk area while talking to the voices coming from her phone's speaker.

Although he acknowledged their connection, Neal was determined to ignore it or fall victim to the games he knew Dana wanted to play.

CHAPTER SEVEN

DANA

DANA GLANCED at herself in her bedroom's standing mirror. She had no idea what type of magic Neal possessed, but his caress inside that cramped elevator had turned her mind and body into a tingling jungle of madness. His touch was an addictive stimulant that kept her from stepping away from him the second time she found herself in his arms.

Maybe the second time was a stumble she orchestrated, but it had gotten her what she wanted. She wanted to see if his touch would be as potent as the first one. Unbeknownst to him, he'd brought out a side of her she had put on ice.

Unfortunately, forcing herself to fall in love with someone was one of the least smart things she'd ever done. Pressure from the men in her family to find a man and settle down, coupled with her own desire to find love and passion, drove her to force relationships. The fake relationships always ended with her being the *"Horrible, heartless, loveless bitch."*

After countless rounds of bad romances, she gave up and opted to let men know her intentions up front, intentions that were the equivalent to her sowing her wild oats. As a result, her unpredictable sex life teamed up with her shady, side life and added up to a hot ass mess. She had dated five men in the past year and had participated in first date sex with all of them, only to be left disappointed and unsatisfied. All she had left to keep her occupied was work.

Her current attempt to find peace in her alone time pulled her out of her thoughts. She was in the midst of pulling off another devious stunt to ditch Neal. She took one last lingering glance back at her house, satisfied that she still had the skills to stride into her freedom when she needed it most. Neal may have gotten the jump on her first escape attempt, but she wasn't one to give up anything easily. Tonight, she had plans, and they didn't involve her hot babysitter.

The biting chill in the air was a minor nuisance compared to her nagging mind repeating how badly she needed to find a lead on the third man who'd participated in her mother's murder. The maddening urges to hunt that she endured would wreak havoc on a relationship if she managed to find success in one. She hated to admit that a relationship would always come second to her need for vengeance, but she accepted the notion.

She parked and exited her car before turning to point her key fob to arm the alarm. She zipped up her black leather jacket, taking the zipper up to her neck to ward off the sprinkling chill that swept her skin in breezy whispers. Her heels sounded hollow against the concrete path along the front of the Turkey Creek Bowling Alley.

Jamie Kavanaugh with his beaty brown eyes and grease slickened hair was a shady lawyer who represented the kinds of assholes she hunted. He was also a backstabbing snitch who she'd blackmailed into being her confidential informant.

Turning a blind eye to murder was among his many bad deeds. Her threats to turn him in to the authorities for the illicit business he'd been conducting on behalf of his clients had done the trick.

He was who'd called her when she'd locked herself in her office bathroom with Neal breathing down her neck. He'd called again a few hours ago, insisting he had information on Luther Drago, her next target.

She didn't trust Jamie any further than she could see him and made sure she'd strapped on extra security in case he'd gotten the balls to initiate a setup. The man would sell out his own mother if the price was right, which had her wondering how he'd survived for as long as he had, dealing with the kinds of monsters she hunted. Maybe his ruthlessness made him a valued asset. However, his information always gave her a credible lead, especially when she reminded him of the jacket of proof, she possessed implicating him in multiple crimes.

After entering the building, she strutted past the counter where three attendants stood in front of a wall of bowling shoes. They set their gazes on her heels until she disappeared from their line of sight. The crush of laughter, mingling conversations, and country music in the background met the sharp sound of bowling balls striking pins.

Jamie's midnight black hair, gleaming as though he'd dyed it with shoe polish, resembled melted plastic beneath the lights blinking, 'Lane 17' above his head. He was in his late forties, but coloring his hair told his age more than if he'd allowed himself to go natural.

A bowling ball sat tucked against his chest. The fake smile on his face when he spotted her was easily recognized. She knew damn well he wasn't happy to see her.

He set the heavy ball in his hands, settled his stance in alignment with the alley, and took measured steps before tossing it towards the pins. He spun and faced her without waiting to see his results.

"Ms. Paxton, nice to see you this evening."

His voice carried over the hum of the surrounding noise and now pop music, Britney Spears, "Toxic" playing in the background.

Dana pursed her lips at him lying his ass off. When she didn't offer up a reply, he followed her example and took a seat, leaving one empty between them.

"Drago would like a meet with you. Tonight." He lifted a brow, his beady light-brown eyes saying a lot more than his words. If Jamie wasn't a necessary evil, she'd kill him on principle alone. His gaze dropped like he could feel the burning contempt she held for him.

"Where?" she asked.

"Here. Go to the ladies' room that's marked 'out of order.' Stall number four."

Her face crinkled, but she didn't comment on the unusual meeting place. If they were setting a trap, she wasn't going down without sending someone or something to hell tonight.

She stood and Jamie followed suit.

"Wait," he called before she turned away. "You're here to negotiate business and not to start any trouble, right?"

The pleading in his gaze let her know he was afraid of her messing up his name with his deadly friends.

She leaned closer to him, her heels putting her at his eye level. "You should be worried about me emptying a dozen or so bullets into your head instead of what your blackhearted friends would think of you."

He jerked away, his wide eyes filled with horror, knowing her well enough to ascertain she'd have no problem making good on her threat. She stepped away but sensed his eyes burning a hole in her back.

Just like when she'd entered the building, the attendants

behind the counter kept their eyes on her heels. They stared so hard, she expected one to offer her a pair of bowling shoes.

While approaching the restroom door, she noticed there was a white sheet of paper taped to it, informing the ladies it was out of order and to use the restroom at the other end of the building.

Dana's hand brushed the metal tip of the pistol shoved down the back of her jeans. Her leather jacket covered the bulge as well as hid her favorite long-blades she felt naked without. She'd appropriately named her blades King and Queen. Depending on her attire she could adjust the custom made sheath so the blades sat aligned with her spine or sat in an X across her back. Tonight they were nestled against her spine. Two extra clips of ammunition and two knives were secured to her body as well.

Dana eased the squeaky bathroom door open with her shoulder. Her steps, though muffled, echoed off the walls as she approached the stall Jamie had indicated. It was the largest and sat against a brick wall. Stepping inside, she took in the shiny, portable metal wall attached to the sturdy brick.

Click. Click.

Her HK VP9 was out and aimed before she had a chance to process that the sound had emanated from the brick portion of the wall inside the stall. It was a secret doorway into some hole-in-the-wall spot she'd have no choice but to enter.

Dana had encountered Drago, with his permanently smug face and deep set guilty dark brown eyes, on a few prior occasions. Thankfully, she'd not met with him face to face.

She crept into the space, using her shoulder to shove the opening further apart. Her pistol led her into the darkness that swallowed its shiny surface as she crept deeper inside.

"Ms. Paxton, there is no need for that weapon," a deep, smooth voice called out. She tightened her grip on her gun. The air around her sizzled with a suffocating energy that ignited her fury and sent her mind into a frenzy of raging thoughts that all screamed *murder.*

"I'll believe that as soon as I'm walking out of here in one piece with my order fulfilled." Her words were forced through clinched teeth to fight the desperate urge she had to kill. What was it about these monsters that set her off so badly she could hardly contain her rage?

A quick rush of wind flew past her face before the door shut behind her and plunged the space into complete darkness. Light footsteps drew closer, and although she was blind, she sensed being surrounded.

Gradually, shadowy sheets of light crept into the room, revealing the five men surrounding her. Drago's face was the first image to come into focus, and it took gut wrenching will power to stop herself from pulling the trigger. That and the fact that her bullet would be wasted on him. She had to bide her time and shoot her shot when the opportunity was right.

"Ms. Danelle Paxton, you have quite the shady reputation."

His gaze dropped with searching ease as he took her in from head to toe.

"You have dipped what I think are pretty toes, based on the rest of you, into a lot of illegal activity over the years. Drugs, high dollar theft, murder, even spent some time in jail. You've been one busy little trouble making bee."

He sounded proud of the fake background she'd built under the Paxton alias.

Little did he know, she was a far worse criminal in her secret legal job.

"A girl's gotta eat," she said, handing her weapon over to one of Drago's human guard dogs who stood there with his palm outstretched, waiting for it.

Drago took in a long-winded sniff with his eyes locked on hers. His tongue passed across his lips several times, reminding her of a hungry dog staring at a steak he was preparing to scarf down.

"Has anyone ever told you that you smell like what heaven must be like?"

"Can we get on with business? I'm not here to gag on your cheesy pick-up lines," she spat at him. He had no idea the kind of restraint it was taking her to stand in the same room with him, let alone look into his murderous eyes.

It wasn't enough that he'd participated in her mother's murder and used humans for snacks. He also had a thirst for committing murder and was getting paid to do it. Being face to face with him without losing her temper, or setting the building on fire, was revealing of how much she had grown over the years and how much control she'd learned to exert over her bloodlust.

"I received your order and the first half of your payment, but instead of the second half in all currency, I'd like something else from you."

He licked his lips again. His men hadn't said a word and stood in place like the trained, murdering dogs they were.

Drago reached into his jacket and the motion had her tensing and taking up a defensive posture.

"Relax Ms. Paxton." He flashed a teasing grin she wanted nothing more than to knock off his face. He retrieved a pen and, without having to ask, one of his men handed over a piece of paper. He scribbled his new payment demands on the paper and handed it over.

"I'd much rather *that* to cover the second half of your payment. If we're in agreement, I'll fulfill your order, and we'll meet at a new location to make the exchange."

She nodded in Drago's direction although his written request had thrown her for a loop—drugs, blood, and a smaller portion of money.

And not just any kind of blood, his monstrous ass wanted a sip of hers.

The drugs he wanted would come from one of the contacts she had imbedded in her built history he'd likely memorized. Thankfully, for her sake, she knew the drug dealer who was as sought after as a billionaire bachelor.

Dana had to get away from Drago now, or all bets were off on her ability to keep her composure. She took a few steps back, lifting the note he'd handed her.

"I'll see you later," she told him before turning away and heading toward the area where she'd entered the room.

"Yes, you will," he replied, but she was too overwhelmed to decipher if his statement held any hints of malice.

She jerked her pistol from the guard while rolling her eyes at his wide, teasing smile. Her body was on the verge of breaking apart from how much energy she needed to control her urge to kill. Thankfully, no one made a move to stop her.

The click of the door sounded, the crack widening the closer she stepped.

Once she exited the building and made it to her car, she sat inside and breathed away the blood lusting urge that plagued her each time she was anywhere near one of the monsters. Her chest heaved, and the cab of her car filled with her loud breaths.

Finally, Dana allowed a smile to creep across her face. She had successfully maneuvered her way into Drago's life, the move giving a whole new meaning to the saying of keeping-your-enemy-close.

A knock sounded on her window, startling her. The spicy ginger scent that followed the knock punched her in the nose even with her window up. Her senses tingled, the urge to kill taking her mind by storm.

Using her speed only got her as far as ripping her gun from the place she'd shoved it down the back of her jeans. The monster outside her window was fast enough to open her door, reach in, and snatch her out by the neck, knocking her gun out of her hand and onto the floor of her car.

Swift punches were delivered to his mid-section, arms, and face, making him reposition his arms around her to stop them from connecting. His grip on her arms would no doubt leave bruises, his fingers pressing so hard into her skin, she was sure he had squeezed down to the bone. He spun her, pinning her back against his chest when she didn't give up her quest to rip out his soul and spit on it.

"You killed my brother, bitch!" He barked the biting words into her ear while holding her from behind, his forearm pressed against her windpipe. "I've been trying to track you down for a year."

His words were winded from the effort she was forcing him to exert to keep her under control. Dana had no idea who held her in his tight grip. She'd encountered more than her fair share of monsters, so this one's decree for vengeance was probably justified.

"If I killed your brother, he deserved it. I don't pull the trigger or sling a blade unless I have justification," she forced out, struggling against his strong hold. The tight grip had her gasping as the force of his strength pushed at her chest and constricted her breathing.

He sniffed her, his nose and the sound of his loud inhale running along her neck before he spun her to face him. His facial features were surprisingly normal. Chiseled jawline, clean shaven, dark short hair. His eyes held his savagery. His wild eyed gaze was an unnaturally violet color that flashed the rage churning inside him.

She spun out of his hold and showed him how careless he was in his handling of her. One of her smaller blades went flying into his chest at a sideways angle, causing him to release her arms and stumble back a few steps.

Dana followed her stab with a forward kick, sending the ball of her foot into his wobbly leg. The sound of his scream, when his knee bone separated from his femur with a loud *snap*, was going to draw attention to the dim parking lot. His rage kept him standing despite the damage he'd suffered.

He rushed her, narrowly missing her with a deadly fist to the face. His punch flew past her view in a blur of light, his pale skin glistening against the night.

The interior of her car, from the door being open, provided enough light for her to glimpse his anger. His sole purpose this night was to end her life. She could almost smell the hate he harbored for her.

"The feeling is mutual," she mouthed to his unspoken hatred.

She countered his movements, shifting her body around to his side, and catching him with another devastating kick to his other leg. He went down hard, but not without taking her with him.

He hadn't anticipated her speed; none of them ever did. You weren't supposed to kick a man while he was down, but this was not a man. It was the bane of her existence.

Sevyn reached behind her neck, past her leather jacket collar to draw one of her long blades. The man, *thing*, made no attempt to beg for his life when his eyes caught sight of the blade. Instead, he glared up at her, the hate in his eyes so strong, she felt it like an unwanted ache. His chin lifted in defiance even as her blade, Queen, swung through the air leaving a *whooshing* sound in its wake.

The blade connected with tissue and bone which caused a hacking sound to echo through the space. The second and third chops sounded off just as loud.

Tonight was supposed to be a peaceful mission, to secure a lead that would guarantee her target and a possible lead to her last. However, she was finding that she had left her fingerprint on more than just her weapons. She had touched enough monsters that some were out hunting for her.

"The hunter has become the hunted," she mouthed to herself while glancing around to make sure no one saw her with a decapitated head, blood still pouring from it, in her hand. All anyone would see was that she'd hacked a man apart, unaware he wasn't even on the human spectrum.

CHAPTER EIGHT

NEAL

NEAL STAYED awake most of the night after discovering that Dana had sneaked away from the house. If only he'd increased his security checks to ensure she didn't try anything.

He understood his mistake came in attempting to preserve her privacy. Instead of entering her room to do a physical check, he would crack the door open and take a quick peek. Now, he feared he had fallen into one of her traps and aided in making her escape easier.

Neal searched every corner of her room before discovering he had just missed her. The loose hangers in her closet continued to swing, and her bed was still warm. Stepping into the hall, it didn't take but a second for him to notice the hallway curtains billowing at the far end of the hall.

Dana had left a crack in the window, and he saw nothing but darkness staring back at him when he peered outside. A light misting of rain came down, carrying with it a late April chill.

He conducted a thorough search of the perimeter of the property and interviewed the guards about what they had observed in the past half-hour without mentioning that Dana was the reason for his questions. As he suspected, none of them were the wiser that she was gone. This was likely her normal routine, slipping away while they were left guarding an empty house.

Neal spent most of the night stressed and searching, and it was only now that he understood why her father had been so firm in his warnings about her nature. She was as slick as motor oil. It wasn't like Neal to lose anyone, yet she'd slipped right through his fingers, even with him steps away, across the hall.

He posted up next to the window she had slipped out of to await her return. He hadn't found any feasible escape routes she could have used and had no idea how she'd made it past her own front yard. The place was as fortified and guarded as a maximum-security prison.

Hours later, and as day began to break, he remained in place at the window. A deep crease dented his forehead. Was that Dana's voice emanating from someplace within the house?

He turned away from the window in time to see her step out of her room laughing into her cell phone. Dressed and ready to start the workday, she flashed a roguish smirk that highlighted her misbehaving ways. Her teasing wave followed.

"Good morning, Mr. Erickson. How did you sleep?"

She knew damn well he hadn't slept, and the teasing glint in her eyes revealed as much.

"I'm doing fine, Miss Diallo. Didn't get much sleep last night, though."

How the hell did she get back into the house?

Neal was at a loss. Dana had not only managed to get away from him, but she'd found a way in and out of the house without anyone noticing. Now, she was acting like nothing had happened.

This would be his first time accepting the offer, but Neal decided to take the invitation to join her and her father for breakfast. He needed to see past Dana's looks to unscramble the mysteries surrounding her.

The devilishness she couldn't keep out of her eyes was almost as telling as the subtle tension that tightened her whole body each time he stared too hard. It was like she knew he was running scenarios of what she was hiding through his head.

Where was she going at night? Had she been sneaking away every night? Was last night the first time he'd noticed? He'd been her personal guard for over two weeks now and expected that she would try something sooner or later. The notion that she could have gone out and gotten killed on his watch was unacceptable.

Her teasing wink found him when he entered the dining room, purposely taunting him.

Why can't I track her?

Neal observed with a pensive eye while she engaged her father in pleasant conversation about his upcoming trip to Afghanistan. William treated his daughter like a princess and was capable to caving to her every whim, only drawing the line on her protection.

Intent on observing more closely, Neal needed to view her from a different perspective. Instead of a wealthy Diallo princess, he thought more along the line of sneaky opportunist. Today, she wore a baby blue skirt suit that, of course, high-lighted her sophisticated elegance.

However, he noticed something she had failed to conceal. A series of large, fresh bruises on her arm. Since the sleeve of her suit jacket was three-quarter length, the bruises peeked from under her left sleeve.

She noticed where his eyes had gone and adjusted her sleeve before glancing at her father to see if he noticed. William never broke their conversation.

Neal decided that he wasn't going to address Dana about the bruises. If she wanted to conduct disappearing acts, he had a few tricks up his sleeves that would stop her in her mysterious tracks.

Dana

After stepping into her office, Dana removed her jacket and took a seat at her desk. Neal had already seen her bruises, so there was no need to hide them. On the drive over, he hadn't mentioned anything about her disappearing on him last night.

She'd been in such a hurry to get ready this morning, she didn't have time to pick out a better outfit and hardly had time to get herself into one. She had spotted Neal waiting at the window during her attempt to sneak back into the house.

Since she had already been late for breakfast with her father, she'd had to make a mad dash to the rear of the house to find an alternate route. Thank goodness she'd been sprinkled with a little supernatural magic that gave her the ability of speed. She appreciated Neal keeping his mouth shut in front of her father because all he would have done was stress and call for more guards.

Standing behind her desk, she gathered the supplies she needed to start her workday. Neal stood on the other side of her desk clocking her every move. It was strange; he didn't appear upset by her actions last night. Instead, she sensed he wanted to know how she had pulled it off. His eyes gradually settled into a squint, making the crease between them form the letter V.

Dana broke eye contact and involuntarily scratched her head, he'd had her thinking too hard. The last thing she needed was him figuring out that she was attracted to him. Neal wasn't going to be as easily swayed to quit as the other guards.

He didn't take his usual seat near the exit today but chose to sit in one of the chairs in front of her desk, studying her. She carried on with the repetitiveness of her daily work routine and found that she was unusually comfortable under his penetrating gaze.

"I've got something for you, Miss Diallo," he said, out of the blue.

Her shoulders dropped on a long-winded sigh. He'd called her Miss Diallo again.

"Please, call me Dana."

She glanced up and, dangling from his finger, were her blue panties.

His blank expression met the surprise she couldn't keep out of her expression or the twisted smile she couldn't keep off her lips.

"I washed and dried them for you, but I can hang on to them if you want. That way, if you have another *accident,* you'll know that I have an extra pair for you. Can't have you running around with no panties on. After all, I am here to protect you in every way that I can."

A smile lifted her cheeks. He was a sneaky quiet storm. She prayed he didn't figure out her secrets before she produced a plan to get him fired.

Her assistant buzzed in a call that drew a little of her attention away from Neal. As she spoke, her gaze remained on him. His chest rose high from the deep sniff he took of her panties before returning them to the pocket of his jeans.

The sight of his deliberate action had caused her to fumble the phone she had picked up, but she recovered without missing a beat in her speech. The last thing she wanted was to talk about financial portfolios when she had something ten times more interesting in front of her.

She continued the brief, placing the call on speaker while reaching to shrug into her jacket.

Neal rounded her desk and assisted her, his closeness a welcome intrusion. However, she wasn't dumb. He had only gotten closer to get a better view of her bruises. Once she concluded her phone conversation, she faced him.

"Let it go, Mr. Erickson. It's not what you think. I'm not being abused or hurt."

It was careless of her to let him see her bruises in the first place. Concern registered in his tight expression, and she didn't understand why the simple gesture roused her curiosity about him.

"Please call me Neal. I'm not here to discourage you from doing whatever it is you believe you need to do. But, if it entails danger, I'd like to help you. It's my job to keep you safe, even if you insist on doing things to put yourself in danger."

Eyes fixed and lips parted, she studied him.

Is he serious?

The mystery surrounding him made her attraction grow stronger with each of their encounters. Now that he admitted that he would follow her into danger, she debated whether she wanted to reveal her secrets to him.

Would he tell my father? Would he try to stop me? Will my secrets get him killed or would he be an unexpected ally?

CHAPTER NINE

DANA

HER OFFICE PHONE, once again, saved Dana from having to respond to Neal. She continued her briefing about investments and numbers, but her mind was on its own course. Every once in a while, she gazed up from her figures to find him studying her. She liked his eyes on her and found it difficult not to react to him staring so intently.

Her garter strap snapped loose from her panty hose, popping against her leg when she adjusted her stance against the front of her desk. Now, she would be forced to hold on to the gossamer hose to keep it from slinking down her leg. Getting off the phone with Mr. Tabor wasn't an option, so she was stuck in her small dilemma.

A wily smile brightened her mood. Neal hadn't left his spot in front of her desk and appeared perfectly content studying her every move.

After muting her phone, she picked up a pen and folder. "Mr. Erickson, will you help me with something, please? I'm fresh out of hands."

He stood. "Yes, Miss Diallo. What do you need?"

The tease in his tone wasn't missed. He was playing along,

but she sensed he had about a thousand scenarios running through his brain on how to keep her under control.

When he stepped in front of her, she used the pen to lift the hem of her skirt and pointed at her hanging garter strap, daring him with her eyes to touch it.

"Will you fix this for me?"

Her confident stance widened before her teeth bit into the tip of the pen. The folder remained in her other hand, a nonessential item she used in her scheming ploy. Getting rid of Neal meant freedom, but he was the first to make her have second thoughts.

Was he standing there considering her request? Did he not care about getting fired? His eyes gave away nothing but confidence while holding her gaze. He lowered his eyes to the hanging strip of fabric with its plastic snap affixed to the tip.

Neal inched closer into her personal space, making her breath hitch. He had distracted her so intensely that it took the sound of her caller's voice, blaring from her speaker, to recapture her attention.

"Miss Diallo, are you there? Did we get disconnected?" Her tongue skimmed across her lips. "I'm here. You'll need to diversify more of your liquid assets to get the kind of results you're seeking."

Neal lowered, taking a bended knee in front of her. Whatever words she was preparing to speak faltered on her parted lips. There gazes met and locked. The action, though simple, caused ripples of anxious sexual energy to flood her system. What was he going to do next?

She drew strength from deep within and managed to continue her briefing with Mr. Tabor. Neal was so close, the warm flow of his breath bounced off her leg. When his hand made contact with her skin, brushing feathery light over her knee, she jumped and quoted the wrong figures.

"I meant one point two million, Mr. Tabor."

Her breathing picked up speed, keeping pace with her amped up heart rate.

"Are you okay, Miss Diallo?" Mr. Tabor asked with genuine concern in his tone.

"I'm fine," was all she managed before tearing her eyes away from Neal's and putting them on his hand slipping past the hem of her skirt and continuing to glide up her leg.

His stroke sent tremors up her back, and his gaze enticed her to keep watching. She was held captive by his smooth touch and the view of his hand disappearing under her skirt was better than watching a sunrise. He didn't lift the material like she expected. Did he know enough about women's lingerie to reconnect her hosiery blindly? She didn't know, but she was game to find out.

Her conversation stalled when Neal reached his other hand between her legs, positioning it to sit flush along the backside of her thigh. Gently, he brushed along her warm flesh, sending pulses of excitement racing through her. The position set his face closer to her throbbing hot center, and she attempted to stifle a gasp but wasn't quick enough to stop it from escaping.

There was no way to swallow the lust he had so quickly built inside her. She cleared her throat, preparing to speak, but her words were sucked into the whirlpool of heat and lust Neal had stirred.

The moment he found the two pieces of material he needed to reconnect, the smirk in his eyes was as big as the one on his sexy lips. His hands maneuvered enticingly under her skirt, spiking her heart rate off the charts. Neal's foreplay was better than some of the mediocre sex she'd endured in the past few years.

It took willpower to control her breathing and a reel of mental chants to stop herself from moaning. She wanted to say, *"To hell with it,"* and ask him to spend time on the area he had burning with desire. His hands danced temptingly around her thigh, brushing dangerously close to her pulsing middle.

Her desire leaked, wet and hot, and had her aching for his hand to explore more than her leg. Her breaths raced in and out, giving sound to her revved-up desire which left her spilling enough heat to warm the building.

She jumped at the knock that sounded at her door. Since she had an open-door policy, no one knocked on her door and waited long before entering. Immediately following the knock, her assistant, Jordan peeked her head in and got an eyeful.

Jordan gripped the door handle more firmly, her wide eyes directed at Neal kneeling in front of Dana. Neal didn't make the situation any better. He peered up, flashing a wide grin at Jordan while Dana stood helpless and frozen in place. She was torn between relinquishing the rush he filled her with and saving her assistant from embarrassment. Her inner voice yelled, *"Push him away!"* but her body wouldn't allow her to mount a protest.

Neal didn't remove his hands, either.

Instead, his smooth tone spilled into the room like they weren't caught in a precarious position. "Miss Diallo didn't have time to get back into her clothes, so she asked me to help her out." He cast a teasing glance up at her before glancing back at Jordan. "Since I'm the devoted help, I couldn't very well leave her half-dressed, now could I?"

It didn't occur to Dana until after he'd made the statement that it sounded like he was confirming they'd been in there fucking. The crimson on Jordan's light brown cheeks spread to her neck.

Despite all the shouting going on in Dana's head, none of it ever crossed her lips. Instead, her eyes dropped to where Neal had placed his hands.

Jordan cleared her throat and responded to Neal with, "Okay, I understand your position," before dragging her eyes up to meet Dana's, the words tumbling quickly from her mouth. "Mr. Tabor said the line went dead. I attempted to reconnect him, but you didn't answer your phone."

"I think I got it," Neal announced to no one in particular. His hand skimmed the hem of her underwear, and Dana nearly passed out. Thank goodness Jordan was at a distance, or she would bear witness to how truly weak Neal was making her.

He removed his hand, finally releasing her from the seductive trance he'd cast. He made a show of ensuring she was put back together properly by brushing the sides of her skirt down and straightening her jacket before stepping back to take one last approving glance.

Dana's voice was low, but she was determined to regain some aspect of control. "Send the call back through, Jordan. I'll pick up. Also, will you print the reports so I can start my net assets value calculations and update my accounts?"

Neal stepped away like nothing inappropriate had occurred, and Dana's eyes followed until he'd returned to his area.

"Sure, no problem," Jordan answered. "I'll get those reports started and send the call back."

Dana was convinced, after *that* display, Neal would be hers. He just didn't know it yet.

Thankfully, it was Jordan who had cracked her office door open. Jordan had been with her since the beginning, and Dana knew enough of her assistant's personality to know the other woman was open-minded. Jordan also knew how to keep a secret.

Once Jordan pulled the door closed, Dana peeked around her desk for Neal, tempted to lock them inside and continue what they started.

CHAPTER TEN

NEAL

AFTER HER ASSISTANT closed the door, the smile that crept across Dana's lips and the expression she'd shot at him spelled out her mischievous intentions. She would have let him continue his quest to explore her body.

Neal had stepped away because the woman was pure temptation dipped in a tub of lust and desire. His heart raced with excitement, and he sat with his eyes closed to calm himself.

Not even the presence of her assistant had stopped him from wrapping his hand around her sexy and silky leg. He berated himself for being so male and uncharacteristically weak. She was a temptress with a capital T. So much so, she broke down every defense he believed he possessed.

She was attracted to him, turned on by him even, but he didn't understand the why behind the attraction. Most women as privileged and as beautiful as her could have anyone.

His scar had been with him for seven years. Seven years, unfortunately, was as far in the past as he could remember. TOP's doctors had run every test imaginable, investigating to find out what had caused his amnesia, but they never found an answer.

As a result, he had no idea where he'd come from, who his family was, or if he even had family. At what TOP had estimated was the age of nineteen, he'd emerged into the world with the scar on his face as the only clue to his past.

Neal assumed he'd be placed in a lab and tested like an animal, but TOP only recruited agents who possessed unique abilities which shattered modern science. The top-secret nature of the agency and the job assignments he received were right in line with him being bound by law not to share his unnatural status with normal society. Besides, he couldn't go around telling people he believed he had the ability to jump through space and time. He'd had to go on numerous rescue missions during his career to break agents out of hospitals and lab research facilities after they'd allowed the wrong person to witness their ability.

The disturbing idea that TOP could be the reason he'd lost his memories in the first place surfaced from time to time, but they had never given him a reason to doubt their purpose of tracking down the monsters of the world and fighting for the good guys. He had so easily latched on to the world they exposed him to, he believed he was built specifically for it.

Dana crossed his mind again, consuming it. There was something special about her he hadn't yet put his finger on. She couldn't see him from where he sat, but he watched her get back to work. What was she up to during the times she managed to get away from him? Where was she going, and how had she gotten those bruises? He wanted to gain her trust rather than force her to tell him her secrets, so he delayed questioning her.

He was deep in thought when he glanced up at her beautiful face. She had appeared out of nowhere again. He was the one missing twice as many years of memories than he'd been alive and harbored a supernatural ability, yet Dana possessed more intrigue. She was standing so close, Neal inched back in his chair, playing it off like he was stretching his legs.

"I would like to go to the jewelry store. I need to pick up a pair of earrings I ordered."

"Sure," he replied and smiled despite lingering thoughts of how much her closeness affected him. "As long as you don't have plans to ditch me while you're there."

Dana didn't reply.

Neal followed her to the parking garage without a word. He preferred her sitting in the back when he drove, but she was the kind of woman who sat where she wanted. Images of his hand under her skirt would force him to fight harder to keep his eyes on the road and off her.

She was the most dangerous distraction he'd ever met, but his instincts also told him that she was so much more than her looks.

CHAPTER ELEVEN

NEAL

NEAL WAS DOING a remarkable job by William Diallo's standard, but he knew better. William left him with a parting brief before his departure to Afghanistan, ensuring Neal would stick around. He repeated himself several times, emotion infusing each syllable of his words. "Keep my baby girl safe, Neal. She means the world to me."

Neal left William's office to prepare for another exhausting night. With her father gone, there was no telling what kind of stunts Dana had up her stylish sleeves. It was going to be impossible to protect her if he didn't find out the secrets that were important enough for her to risk her life.

She hadn't used either of the two cars she owned in the garage, so someone was either picking her up, or she was hiding another method of transportation. After discovering her first disappearing act, his last three attempts at following her had been a bust. He'd lost her trail even when he spotted her sneaking through the darkness. No one he knew, unless they were on the supernatural spectrum, possessed the ability to vanish without tech. He watched the woman like a hawk and had never picked up anything that suggested she was more than just human.

He'd walked the perimeter of the property, several times, attempting to figure out how she had plotted her escape routes and gone unnoticed by the guards.

Neil put on his all-black stealth wear, filled his backpack with a few of his high-tech spy toys, and prepared for his fourth attempt to catch the sneaky seductress tonight.

When he turned on the reflective properties of his jumpsuit and put on his hood, he could literally go undetected in darkness and in dim lighting. The suit acted as a mirror, reflecting the night back into the atmosphere, making its occupant virtually invisible.

Did Dana have access to the same type of technology? It would explain her ability to disappear. Though difficult to prove, the idea that she was more than human was starting to sound more plausible. As far as he knew, there weren't many of his kind roaming the planet, if you could classify him as *a kind*.

He eased past the guards without so much as a loose twig breaking and faded into the darkness to the inside of the fence line at the front of the house. Dana was forcing him to treat her like a target, one who harbored as many secrets as the agency that employed him.

It was time he unleashed his training on her. He was also willing to use his *ability* if it came down to it. The way things were unfolding, it was likely the only way he could catch her and get answers. However, explaining teleportation would be difficult if she caught him.

After about a thirty-minute wait, his night vision gear picked up what could have been a person. The object moved as a blur, making him adjust his gear twice before it fell out of sight. Was it Dana?

There it was again, a blip of movement through his lenses.

He adjusted his vision settings once more to make sure he'd

seen a person and not shadows of dancing light. Hearing the quick thump of footsteps and not seeing what made the sound left his eyes wide and searching. His head swiveled in every direction.

He removed his night goggles in time to see a figure leap across the area where he squatted. Whatever it was, it moved so fast the wind gust swept the loose leaves of the shrubs into his face. He targeted this area because it was the one spot he'd found a partial shoe print.

The faint but unmistakable fragrance of Dana's perfume left a trail and helped expose at least one of her secrets. The figure he thought he'd seen, the one that moved too fast for him to track, *was* Dana. He hadn't a clue as to how she pulled it off, but it was a secret he added to the list of mysteries he was figuring out about her.

She hadn't noticed him hunkered near the fence, thanks to the stealth gear. The gear was also designed to conceal his heat signature from other tech devices. If there was better spyware out there, TOP found out about it and either acquired it or duplicated it.

He stood, listening, and searching. How had she gotten across the ten-foot metal fence? He didn't have time to waste figuring it out. To track her further than the front yard, he had to keep moving.

Determined not to lose her, he got himself to the other side of the fence in time to pick up a familiar sound. The crunch of rocks breaking against pavement and the unpleasant intake of exhaust fumes alerted that a car was on the move.

The sound of rolling tires suggested she hadn't gotten far enough away for him to lose her trail. Adjusting his night gear, he picked up the heat signature of a small, dark car traveling swiftly away. Following a nearly invisible car wasn't an easy task. He had to remain far enough in the rear that Dana didn't see him trailing her.

When she was far enough away from the house, the car's headlights snapped on and nearly blinded him. He discarded the night goggles and kept up his pursuit, using the residual light from her taillights to stay on the road. A thousand questions nagged him, but he had no intention of losing sight of the diplomat's mysterious daughter. This was the closest he'd gotten to seeing what she was truly up to on her secret missions.

If Dana caught him, he imagined he would have a difficult time explaining how he was trailing her car on foot. Based on what he believed he'd seen of her through his lenses, she had some explaining to do as well.

Neal followed Dana for nearly forty minutes, pausing only long enough to observe their surroundings. They ended up on the outskirts of the city at the Lamy Bridge. The bridge hadn't been in use for years, so Mother Nature was taking it back. Vines and all manner of shrubbery were staking their claim, wrapping their willowy limbs around the thick rusted metal, and clinging on for dear life.

The bridge was decommissioned and likely scheduled for demolition. It was the perfect place to conduct illegal business if that was what Dana was doing. The moon peeked through the clouds and gave the scene an eerie vibe. A few shimmering rays of moonlight lit the dark water below the bridge, making it dance and wave with life. At a distance, the bridge swayed, hanging by tethered cables stretched and ready to snap.

Dana rolled past reflective warnings and caution signs meant to stop access onto the bridge. She drove cautiously, traversing a steep incline until she reached a leveling point at the center of the unsafe passage.

The few lights that scarcely illuminated the area revealed her driving an all-black compact car. The reflective property of the car's paint job made it, like his suit, appear invisible at certain angles.

He learned about the paint and many other tech advances that the government kept from public knowledge and use. Working for TOP, he owned equipment the rest of the world would never know existed. Since Dana was surrounded by secrets and her father had ties to the government, did she have special access privileges to the same type of equipment?

He trekked closer to where she parked without rousing her suspicion. She sat in the running car waiting for someone, and he wasn't going anywhere until he saw who she was about to meet.

Once Neal located the perfect spot, he climbed atop one of the bridge's wide beams and positioned his body flat on his stomach, facing Dana's position. His head snapped up at an approaching vehicle. Concern climbed into his body and settled in as deep as his bones.

The dim lighting revealed a dark colored Hummer. It drove up slowly, facing Dana's car, and sat running for a stressful minute before the engine was shut off.

Five men exited the vehicle, all armed, none making attempts to hide their weapons.

Neal carried a holstered nine-millimeter but was glad he'd left the house prepared and brought his sniper rifle too.

He unslung it from his back and used the edge of an adjacent beam to hold the weapon in place. As soon as he zoomed in on the men, he found that the dim lighting hadn't deceived his eyes. They were prepared for battle, an indication that this meeting was not going to be a friendly one.

CHAPTER TWELVE

NEAL

DANA EXITED HER VEHICLE, her heels echoing across the concrete as she stepped around to the front of her car.

What is she doing?

Was she wearing those heels when she jumped the fence back at her house and moving too fast for him to track properly? The only time Neal recalled seeing her without a pair of heels on was when she was in bed. She was dressed in an all-black, tight-fitting leather jacket and pants set that reminded him of a sexy superhero.

Is she wearing a wig?

He'd never seen her with her hair down, but the neat bun she preferred led him to believe it was longer than the short bob cut she was now sporting. She stopped in front of who must have been the leader of the group.

The man stepped closer, closing the space between them, and his men followed like he controlled them all by remote. They hadn't taken out their weapons, but their hands rested on the cold steel.

Was he reading this situation wrong or did those men appear threatened by Dana? Their tight postures carried enough tension that any movement, when they did move, was stiff and robotic. And the way they would not take their eyes off her help feed Neal's own tension about this whole situation. What had Dana gotten herself into?

How could she be naïve enough to meet these unsavory-looking characters alone, at night, and in a location where no one could hear her if she needed help? A location where she could be easily killed and disposed of. How was he supposed to protect her if these were the kinds of situations she subjected herself to?

The leader's voice carried across the bridge, a dreary echo that harbored the worst sinner's intent. "Ms. Paxton, where is your backup? You're either the bravest woman I've met or the most stupid. You do know we're dangerous men?"

"I know you're dangerous, *Drago*, but I'm not afraid of you, or your men," she replied.

Although he couldn't see her face clearly, Neal sensed a smile in the condescending tone of Dana's voice and the teasing way she'd dragged out the man's name.

He also noticed she'd been addressed as Ms. Paxton, an alias. Hearing her address the man as Drago shifted his already revved up heart rate to a higher gear.

It can't be him.

The government had been after Luther Drago for years. He was so elusive, agents speculated that he may have the ability to shape-shift, although shapeshifters were extinct according to books he'd found in TOP's supernatural history library.

It didn't take but a second for Neal to zoom in on the man's shadowed face, and his heart shifted another gear. What Neal couldn't understand was how Dana had gotten involved with someone like Drago.

He aimed at Drago's head. Logically, if he killed Drago, the rest of his crew would have time to hurt or kill Dana. The men's stiff postures and the way they stared suggested they were intent on doing her harm.

The sound of Dana's voice sailed across the bridge. "Did you fulfill my order and bring me what I asked for?"

Drago motioned at one of his men who stepped to the rear of their SUV and returned dragging a large, wheeled chest. He placed the chest between Dana and Drago, but closer to Drago's feet. Dana approached and bent low to inspect what was inside the chest. From Neal's vantage point, there was a body inside, but he couldn't be sure.

"You brought the rest of my payment? It's your turn to give me what I want," Drago demanded with a quick wave of his fingers.

Dana picked up a dark briefcase that Neal hadn't noticed sitting within the shadows in the front of her car. She handed it to one of Drago's men who opened it and leaned in to inspect what was inside the case. Drago's smile grew wide at the confirmation before a sharp frown cut the grin short.

"Where is the rest?" he asked, eyeing Dana up and down.

With no regard for the weapons that were clearly visible, she aimed her thumb across her shoulder at her car.

At her movement, the men gripped their weapons tighter, preparing to shoot if she tried anything. She waved them off dismissively like they were in *her* way. The men glanced at each other, probably asking themselves the same question swimming around in his mind.

Is she crazy?

"Will you have one of your men help me drag this chest to my trunk. I need to retrieve your other case from there. I don't want to mess up my manicure getting that thing into my car."

She aimed a finger at the large chest sitting at her feet.

Is she seriously talking about her manicure right now?

Drago snapped his fingers across his shoulder and pointed to one of his men. The one who must have been the lowest ranking in the group stepped forward and began dragging the chest to the back of Dana's car while the rest of the men stared.

Confusion had Neal frowning, his face tensing into a tight knot. He didn't understand how Dana was walking around like she didn't have weapons semi-drawn on her. She opened the hatch of her car and retrieved another briefcase, but remained at the rear of her car, waiting for the man to arrive with her chest.

Drago had his phone lifted to his ear and Neal didn't know if he'd answered it, made a call, or if the person he was currently talking to had listened to the exchange he'd been engaged in with Dana the entire time.

Upon her return, Drago aimed a long threatening stare her way.

"I just received an update on you," he said, shaking an accusatory finger in her face. "You're not who you say you are. Don't you fucking try anything either because I've had a man posted here for hours before you arrived." He growled his words at her before he released a teasing round of laughter. "My man told me you were stupid enough to come out here alone with no backup."

Neal used his scope, the instrument strengthening his vision and illuminating the darkness to allow him to search for the extra man Drago mentioned. Thankfully, his stealth gear had kept him from being spotted when he'd followed Dana onto the bridge.

Dana shrugged like the words she'd been threatened with didn't mean a thing. "I came to do business and couldn't care less about being alone here with you and your men."

Neal interpreted the threat in Drago's tone and sensed the danger tensing his posture without his scope.

Drago pointed towards the back of her car. "Why did you have us kill him, anyway? He was a nobody."

He must have been speaking of the body in the chest Dana

traded him for.

She closed the space between them, getting in the man's face. "The one inside the chest, he was my target. He's the lucky one."

Neal didn't know what to think. The tension in Drago's face and body drew tighter, and he appeared as confused as Neal felt.

"I can't wait to rid this world of things like you," she spat at him.

Neal's confusion was a live wire inside his brain.

Things?

After her comment, an unholy growl filled the air, making the hairs on Neal's neck stand and the sensation of ice race up his back. Spying through his scope, he searched for what made the bloodcurdling wail, and his sights landed right back on Drago. The howl was coming from him, and it didn't sound human.

Drago's voice roared across the bridge, casting bizarre echoes before his dangerous eyes roamed the expanse of Dana's body, like a wolf stalking prey.

"You're so damn sexy. I almost hate to kill you. But I can't wait to taste you. You smell fucking delicious. The first time I got a whiff of your scent, I wanted to rip into one of your veins so badly, I'd had to allow our meeting to be cut short. Now, I finally know why your scent caught me off guard."

Neal was struck dumb, an irritating feeling he rarely experienced. Drago was talking of killing Dana and ripping into her veins. Yet, she was *smiling* at him.

What the hell is wrong with her? What the fuck is going on?

While he struggled to make sense of Drago's words, he figured he'd better get prepared to start shooting since Dana refused to take the man's threats seriously.

Drago executed a circling hand gesture to his men before continuing his speech. "I can't believe you were stupid enough to meet with a bunch of killers, alone. You do know who I am, don't you? I mean, *really* know who I am. I can't be touched. I'm

Mr. Untouchable to the authorities, and now that I know you know my secret, I have no choice but to kill you."

Dana's teasing giggle put a deeper crease in Neal's forehead. "Like I said before, I'm not afraid of you, Drago. You're the one who should be afraid. You should have practiced carrying a weapon instead of relying on your goons because, without one, you leave yourself vulnerable to people like me."

With his eyes more adjusted to the dim lighting, Neal observed Drago's eyes go wide and turn a blazing shade of red.

"You're one crazy bitch," he spat at Dana.

Just as Drago positioned his lips to speak again, a gun went *pop, pop, pop, pop* in rapid succession.

CHAPTER THIRTEEN

NEAL

NEAL'S HEART STOPPED. He feared Dana was shot, until he saw her with a gun aimed at Drago's forehead with the muzzle kissing his flesh. Since she wasn't harmed, his head snapped in every direction, searching to figure out what just happened. He sat behind a sniper rifle, yet he hadn't had time to react or to shoot. It didn't take him long to find that Dana had been the one doing the shooting.

Apparently, when she went to her trunk, the case wasn't all she'd taken from it. Drago's entire crew was laid out, all lifeless with a single gunshot wound to the center of their foreheads. They probably had no idea that their lives had been in jeopardy.

Drago stood in front of Dana, his eyes continuing to glow an unnatural red that pierced the darkness like a dim laser.

Neal remained rooted in place while the scene unfolding in front of him kept his eyes roaming and his trigger finger ready.

The sound of the shot was no more than a hiss before the impact of the bullet, a warning shot, struck the ground near Dana's foot. It came from the hidden man Drago had spoken of, letting Dana know Drago still had protection.

Dana's next move baffled Neal's mind and left him questioning who she was and, more importantly, *what* she was. He'd never seen a human move so fast. He didn't have time to process the number of moves it had taken her to get behind Drago and use him as her shield while the muzzle of her pistol kissed the side of his temple.

Neal was starting to understand the reason she favored wearing heels. Right now, they made her closer to Drago's height, which gave her better maneuverability and aim advantage on the sniper. The toe-curling growl pouring from Drago's throat was otherworldly, a sound that scraped at his nerves like nails on a chalkboard.

Dana yelled into the night at the unseen sniper, "If you're smart, you'll reveal yourself. If you know who I am, I'm sure you know that I will not hesitate to chop this bastard's head off and burn it."

Neal was now certain of one thing; Dana was capable of handling herself. She was dangerous and so incredibly fast; her movements blew his mind. He'd searched and hadn't spotted anyone, but she appeared to sense where Drago's last man was hidden.

Seconds later, the man came out shooting, and Dana didn't hesitate to use Drago as her body armor. Slug after slug of automatic weapons fire went into his body. The hard impact of each bullet sent his body slamming harshly against the front of hers. They stumbled back with each deadly blow, Drago screaming for the man to hold his fire.

Neal had the shadowy figure in his sights now. With Dana's life in jeopardy, he didn't hesitate to send a round into the sniper's head, splitting it like a watermelon blown apart by a stick of dynamite.

Dana spun with a howling Drago in her grasp, attempting to figure out who had dropped the sniper. While she yelled for him to reveal himself, Neal's mind was being drawn in another direction. Hadn't he seen Drago take at least five slugs?

Why hasn't he dropped yet?

Dana and Drago faced his direction now.

"If you don't want to die, I suggest you show yourself."

"Dana don't shoot! It's me, Neal!" he shouted.

The nightmarish frown on her face dropped when she recognized his voice.

Neal adjusted his rifle and climbed down from his perch. Stepping from the darkness, his eyes landed on the infamous Drago. The man was literally chock-full of holes, but there he stood with only a few drops of blood dirtying his cream-colored shirt.

Dana was mostly blocked by Drago's body, but he fully noticed now the short-styled wig that sat lopsided atop her head from her struggle with Drago. He needed her to explain this situation before his brain exploded.

They stared at each other for a paused moment, long enough for Drago to deliver a blow to her gun hand. The impact of the blow sent her pistol clattering to the ground, and the two of them struggled for dominance.

Drago bucked like a wild horse and moved so fast; Neal's eyes could hardly keep up with him. Whatever speed-enhancing ability he had, Dana possessed it as well. Neal caught enough to know that she had taken a blow to the face before she regained control. It didn't take her but a few seconds to get the fast-moving man back in her grips.

Neal's brows lifted high when Dana twisted the man's neck with speed, strength, and precision, producing a sickening crack of bone. He was impressed and, oddly, turned on at the same time.

Drago's limp body dropped to the ground like a sack of rotten potatoes.

Neal's eyes swept Dana's for answers while she stepped across the body to retrieve her gun. Once she had it in her hands, she took a few steps back, aimed, and sent two slugs into

Drago's chest and two into his head. Apparently, dead wasn't dead enough. She wanted him dead to the tenth power.

Neal was finally starting to understand the statement Dana had expressed in one of their earlier conversations. *"The scariest people never reveal to you how scary they are. They show you right before they take your life."*

The wicked backhand of realization smacked him in the face. Dana was talking about herself.

She marched with purpose towards the open hatchback of her car. After seeing her shoot five men without remorse, Neal glanced at the bodies riddled with bullets while she rummaged through her trunk. The words he was set to speak faltered when she marched away from the trunk with a sword.

What is she going to do with that big ass designer knife?

Neal's mind burned with interest to see what she would do next. If the sword was any indication, she wasn't done with Drago. Just as he'd assumed she would, she returned to the lifeless body. Standing over him, she raised the sword high above her head, preparing to hack him into pieces.

As if a moment of clarity hit her, she glanced up, allowing her gaze to meet his. "I'll explain this to you later, but I have to take his head. This bastard isn't dead."

The first chop went halfway through Drago's neck, sending squirts of blood a couple of feet into the air. The chop opened his neck enough to reveal fragments of bone and chunks of unidentifiable parts. Not much blood seeped from his bullet wounds, but it now gushed onto the dirty pavement from his neck.

The second chop ripped through more of the flesh connecting Drago's head to his body before the metal hit the pavement beneath, causing a spark to flicker from the force of the blow. Neal stood in place, unwilling to interrupt the show. She was fucking Drago up like she was fulfilling a personal vendetta.

Although Neal didn't understand the emotions feeding her brutality, he believed Drago deserved every bit of her rage. He had been shot at least nine times, and Dana had snapped his neck. How could he not have been dead?

Neal watched, maybe a little too eagerly, to see the end results. Dana's show was one for the record books. She'd not stopped swinging until she'd hacked the man's head clean off his body. He glanced around once more, taking in the dark figures laid out and lifeless on the pavement. What would her explanation be for killing five men and believing she needed to hack one of them into pieces? He couldn't wait to hear the history of how she had ended up here.

Drago had been a target on TOP's secret radar for nearly five years, so he didn't feel bad about his death. It was the manner in which Dana delivered it that kept pulling at his interest, or was it concern?

His brow lifted in keen observation at her with the man's head in her hand. She'd gotten a hold of Drago's shoulder-length tresses, so the head dangled from her fingers like a gory chandelier.

A light mist of rain bathed the area with an ominous, foggy tint that converted the scene into what felt like an alternate reality. When Dana took a step in his direction, Neal attempted to access her state of mind.

"I finally got you, you bastard," she mouthed at the head, lifting her chest in triumph. The sound of her heels tapping the pavement was all he could make sense of while his eyes chased her movement. She stepped past him and headed to the rear of her car again.

What are her intentions for that head?

He tilted his head in thought, itching for answers but knowing it was best to be patient.

She sat the head down and beckoned for him. "Neal, will you help me with this please?"

There is a logical explanation, Neal attempted to convince himself. Drago, as far as he knew from his files, was listed as supernatural but with no identifying ability. Dana obviously knew a lot more about Drago than what was recorded in his files.

What if she really was a little off her rocker? He'd seen agents lose it due to the unusual physical and mental demands of their jobs. Dana was a civilian who'd somehow gotten involved with a mass murderer on TOP's kill list.

How?

He assisted Dana in maneuvering the body in the chest to make room for the head. She picked up the head and stuffed it inside before slamming the chest shut and adjusting it inside the compact space of her trunk.

"I'm not crazy," she felt the need to say due to him constantly eyeballing her. Considering what he'd just witnessed and the crazy glint flashing in her unblinking gaze, Neal wasn't sure about her mental stability at this moment.

Two months of answers couldn't have explained what he'd just participated in and witnessed. He worked for an agency that had groomed him to accept that strange was the new norm, and it was the key to his open minded demeanor.

"You killed five people and hacked one's head off. Why?" he asked. His tone was calm while his need-to-know was ravenous.

Dana placed her hand on the car's hatchback. "I'll explain once we get out of here. All I ask is that you keep an open mind."

She slammed the hatch shut with thundering finality, walked around, and climbed into the driver's seat.

Fuck!

Still, no answers.

Neal believed his mind couldn't be any more open. However, needing to know how a wealthy diplomat's daughter, one that he was supposed to be protecting, had gotten so deeply involved with aspects of his world had him on edge.

He'd seen all sorts of unimaginable scenes in the line of duty, but this one was becoming one of his most baffling to process without answers.

What the fuck was she going to do with that head? Cook it? Eat it or make an ornament out of it?

CHAPTER FOURTEEN

NEAL

Since Dana informed that she would explain later, Neal refrained from asking questions right away. However, the amount of confusion he harbored made him change his mind quickly.

"How were you and Drago able to move so fast? Do you have an undocumented ability of some sort? Is it something you take that makes you move fast? There is no way anyone knows what you can do, or they would lock you in a lab and study you or clone you."

Her face remained aimed straight ahead, her body momentarily frozen while dancing shadows outside her window increased the intensity of her profile.

"I operate under the codename Sevyn. When I wear the wig, I'm her, or I have gone under." She jerked the damp wig off and sat it on the center console. "I was given the name Sevyn by another woman like me. We were working a case together and had no choice but to disclose our secret strengths to each other in order to survive. But, even before that, we sensed there was something extra within us. The same way I sense something in you, Neal."

His back stiffened and remained in a tight knot.

"She and I, we don't have the same ability, but she has a special gift, nonetheless. When we were working together, she pointed out that I moved seven times faster than the average person. Why seven times faster, I don't know, but she started calling me Sevyn. I liked the name, so I kept it. We call her Smoke. Anyway, I'm not sure how I'm able to move so fast. It all started after my mother was murdered. It was like the horrific incident sparked something in me."

Neal dragged in long breaths and blew them out with ease to draw in some patience. Dana couldn't talk fast enough to tell him all he wanted to know.

"I'm assuming you haven't told many people, if anyone, about your special gift or secret job? You keep that part of yourself hidden away until you need to use it? Do people usually die when Sevyn comes out?"

Silence filled the space before her seat's leather squeaked under her movement.

"Before I give you more answers, I have to ask...are you not freaked out about what you just saw or what I'm telling you? You're handling this with more ease than I would have expected."

He shrugged. "This job sometimes doesn't leave me much room to freak out. Mentally and physically, I've always been able to handle my share of chaos. The need to know the answers, and the explanation behind the scenes is what kills me."

Silence filled the cab of the small car once more. The tight, suffocating space was alive with unanswered questions although Dana seemed at peace with chopping off heads and killing groups of people.

The lights from the dashboard illuminated her face with an unnatural glow. He stared at her image, gathering his thoughts to put them in logical sequence.

"You took out Luther Drago." He spit the statement out. "The government has been after him for years and you have his head in your trunk."

Dana didn't say anything for a long while before she asked, "How do you know his name? How do you know who the government wants? You're not just some random protection officer, are you? You also killed someone without a second thought and with a sniper rifle. And dare I ask, how were you able to track me to that location?"

Neal was determined to find answers, and Dana was taking her time about giving them.

"You, first. I need more answers. I'm supposed to be *your* protection, remember."

He wasn't willing to lay his cards out on the table until he saw more of hers. By naming Drago, he was divulging to her that he knew top secret government information. She operated under a code name and had the inside track to agents and supernatural criminals. Would she connect the dots and reach the same conclusion that had formed in his head?

She dragged in a deep breath before releasing it on a long exhale. "I have been doing this, officially, for four years now. I capture or kill for the government, cleaning their list that involve mostly Drago's kind. But you're not off the hook, either. It didn't take me long to figure out that you weren't the average, everyday bodyguard. How do you know who Luther Drago is?"

He stared straight ahead, his penetrating gaze pushing through the darkness. Deflection probably wasn't going to work this time. He needed to give up something, but he had never shared anything other than assignment details with other agents.

"You're a spy for the government? Is that why you work so hard to keep secrets from your family? Is that why you couldn't tell me anything?"

"Yes," she replied. "And now I need you to keep my secret.

My rich girl persona is the perfect cover. Technically, I don't exist in this world. If something ever happens to me, I'm well aware they'll make it look like an accident. Now, it's your turn."

Should he tell her that he believed they were likely a part of the same team? She wasn't going to believe him.

"What if I told you it's possible that we work under the same program?"

He sensed her assessing him in the dark. He was tempted to tell her to put her eyes back on the road, but she turned back in time to relieve his stress.

"It would be too much of a coincidence and could mean my father knows about the secret circles I run in, which puts his life in serious danger."

Her tone cast hollow, like she was talking to herself and thinking at the same time. Neal doubted her father knew about her double life, or he'd have an army of protection surrounding her twenty-four hours a day.

"Your father knows you have secrets, but I don't believe he knows who you work for. He doesn't even know who *I* truly work for. The program I work under is smart and strategic in their planning. Agents are assigned jobs depending on their skills and training level, and based on what I've witnessed tonight, they may also be given assignments based on their *ability*. If my agency believed a fellow agent needed help or should be spied on, they will find a way to put us together."

"If we work for the same type of agency, what sector do you work for?"

Neal cleared his throat. "I work for TOP, and they don't have sectors. They create them."

The seat belt snapped against his chest, the thick nylon pressing hard into his flesh as the sound of screeching tires reached his ears. His head flew off the headrest with a quick lurch that had him reaching out and gripping the dashboard and door panel.

"I take it you just gave me whiplash because we truly do work for the same team?"

Her head shook rapidly. "There's no way. As far as I know, there are only about five-hundred TOP agents in the country, at any given time. The job is so dangerous, you damn near have to qualify as crazy for them to recruit you." She leaned closer, putting her eyes level with his. "Prove it. Tell me some things a TOP agent would know."

There was a genuine spark in his smile for the first time. "Only a member of TOP would be doing some of the dangerous and homicidal shit I just witnessed. I still don't understand the head thing, although TOP only gets involved in cases that are not normal. I have seen many things I can't explain, but tonight went in a whole different direction of strange."

He tilted his head in thought.

"You haven't done it yet, but you'll call a cleanup crew to clear the bridge. And before day breaks, the scene will be so clean that no one will know that you or anyone was there."

Neal snapped his finger, remembering something else.

"The body you have in the chest will be picked up by one of the agency's body snatchers. Like the bridge, all you have to do is provide them with a set of grid coordinates. Since he was likely on TOP's kill list, they will build their own crime scene to make his death a believable natural or accidental occurrence. Like I said before, if the agency wants us together for whatever reason, they will make it happen. I didn't get this assignment out of the blue for nothing."

Dana grew unusually quiet, processing the fact that they worked in the same underworld, and TOP was about as far under as one could get without falling into another dimension.

She retrieved her phone, hit one button, and started talking. "Clear Sevyn, 47-6262 North, 122.3359 West. Put the headless one on ice."

After she hung up the phone, Neal sensed her probing eyes on him. Why did she want Drago's dead body on ice?

"You're hiding an ability," she stated, sounding sure. "If I'm going to tell you all my secrets, you need to come clean. I sensed something different in you the moment we met."

Neal didn't like being put on the spot.

"If you tell me why you took the head, I'll tell you more of my secrets."

As if on cue, a guttural groan rattled off, leaving a light vibration rolling through the cab of the car. Neal's head whipped around, staring into the blackness in the rear of the car. He managed a calm and even tone.

"What is that? Please tell me that wasn't that head making that noise?"

CHAPTER FIFTEEN

NEAL

NEAL'S wide-eyed expectant glare was zeroed in on Dana while she silently contemplated her next words. Her throat cleared after another rumbling moan sounded. "Yes, that's the head moaning and the reason I took it. I have killed that thing two times already. It took me a while to figure out that his kind only stays dead when you separate the head from the body and burn it. His kind is what killed my mother. He was one of the five who murdered her."

Dana's knuckles strained against her skin she gripped the steering wheel so tight.

"The government has a way of finding answers. When they found out I, as a teen, was bold enough to start tracking down what killed my mother, they picked me up. They weren't bothered that I was committing crimes, but more interested in how I'd made repeated contact with the monsters I was hunting and lived to talk about it. Long story short, the government recruited and trained me. They know I have a secret ability, and likely saw me using it before they pulled me in."

Neal didn't doubt her logic. TOP took on the kinds of top-secret cases that never saw the light of day, but this, the living undead, pushed him into another level, or perhaps section of the organization.

"I saw Drago take five shots from his own man, and four shots from your gun. You snapped his neck and chopped off his head. You've admitted to killing him twice before now. What the hell is he?"

"The government knows they exist, just as they know people like you and me exist. I don't know what they are, and I don't like what others call them because I refuse to accept that they exist."

As much as Neal wanted to remind her that they operated in and around the abnormal, he didn't because there were things, including the thing in the back of her car that he hadn't believed existed either. He spun in his seat, glancing back once more.

"What is that? I've mainly been assigned missions that involved me rescuing other agents from places deemed impenetrable. I've hunted down criminals that were gifted at manipulating science and space and time in order to commit their heinous crimes. Ones who killed through telepathy. I've even encountered a *rixie* that had the ability to kill humans. Her goal was to kill the four implicated in her murder before discovering that she enjoyed killing and started a murder spree that spanned over twenty years. However, the head of the thing you have in the chest is new to me, not something I've encountered in my years of working for TOP."

Dana's shoulders hunched. "A bullet to the heart and head puts them down, but they won't stay down for long. I discovered a year ago, by accident, that burning their heads will kill them when it's separated from their bodies. The first time I killed Drago was three years ago. I blew up his car. When I went after his buddy months later, Drago was walking around like nothing had happened. I've been hunting the men who murdered my mother for nearly nine years. I've killed those same men repeatedly, ignorant to the fact that they regenerate and heal so rapidly, they are almost indestructible."

What is he?

"Each time they re-emerged after I assumed I killed them, I wondered if I was crazy or seeing a ghost. Since I know how to kill them now, I've killed two. Drago will be the third. Once I'm done with him, I'll track the last."

She still hadn't provided a name for what she suspected they were. He had a theory, but he wanted her words.

"I also discovered they have a strange attraction to me, and I'm not sure if it's the way I smell or my appearance, but I believe I'm a temporary distraction for them. I don't know which, but they have made attempts to bite me or eat me. When I interact with them, my need to kill them becomes so intense, it's difficult to control the urge."

Which of his thousand questions should he ask first?

"Drago is obviously not human and, based on the way you handled him, you know what he is. The government is obviously all over something like this, studying and testing it, but how have I not encountered this before now?"

Dana released a long-winded sigh. "The government has been privy to this type of thing long before we got here and will be long after we're gone. They work hard to keep shit like this from the media and normal society, so what makes you think they can't keep whatever they want from us as well? As long as more people, us, and civilians, are in the dark than not, they consider it a job well done."

It was true, but she was avoiding his questions. The agency would build crime scenes, doctor video evidence of supernatural sightings, and pay people off. They also employed a team of scientist whose jobs were to explain with science that which couldn't be explained.

"They hire people like you and me who don't have a problem keeping shit like this hidden because we also have something to hide. Why do you think they never bothered asking us to show them our unique ability? They already know what we can do. By the time they make contact with us, they have dug so deep into our pasts that they know we haven't harmed an innocent, and that they can trust us to a certain point.

"When have you ever been asked how often you use your ability on the job? However, the fact that we have an ability is the only reason we were hired in the first place. I'm not saying I don't trust TOP's mission because I've never caught or killed anyone who wasn't a murderer. They make sure I have every tool at my disposal to do thorough research before I pull the trigger. But you have to consider, they don't force us to show them one of our most intimate secrets because it makes us less likely to explore them any deeper."

She had a point, and Neal, as well as other agents had made multiple attempts to explore the agency deeper but ended up like a dog chasing its tail. Her mentioning it meant that she had done some exploring herself.

He hoped she didn't think he'd forgotten that she had yet to give a name to the creature in the trunk of her car moaning a twisted opera solo. Was it a zombie or another supernatural creature the government was keeping under wraps?

"TOP hired and trained me to take out or catch targets like that thing when they pose a deadly threat to normal society. In return for cleaning the streets of their kind, they give me the license and means to hunt down the ones who murdered my mother. The asshole back there just happened to be on both our kill lists."

She glanced at him, nodding absently. "They knew about my mother's murder, and sometimes I get the sense that they know more than even I know. What other agency do you know about that will allow their employee to freely hunt and kill what murdered her mother? They could have saved me years of hunting and disclosed to me how to permanently kill the monsters, but until I figured it out on my own, my task had always been to turn the heads in to one contact and the rest of the body into another. I'm convinced that they were conducting research and probably still are on the monsters I captured for them."

She had one hell of a point. The agency was as big a mystery as the unexplored underworld they were opening to them. However, he wouldn't have volunteered to work for them if he didn't believe in the work he was doing and their agenda. They were all trained to preserve and protect human life above their own and above the lives of other supernatural's.

"According to his file, Drago's killed over twenty people that we know about. The four human guards working for him tonight have killed just as many people on Drago's behalf." She aimed a finger across her shoulder and the frown of irritation on her faced deepened.

"I had to find a way to get Drago to trust me, so I hired him to kill one of my targets. In exchange for killing my target, he wanted, of all things, vials of my blood. He claimed it was for research. I, of course, pretended like I didn't know why he wanted it. I was almost tempted to stand around and see what would happen if he drank the acid I'd put in those vials instead of blood."

Dana was vicious, calm under pressure, and deadly. Definitely a TOP agent.

"The second case I gave Drago was filled with cocaine and money. His kind don't become addicts like humans. Drugs help them stave off their thirst for blood. We take aspirin for headaches. They take drugs for their blood-aches."

Neal didn't miss how reluctant Dana was to give a name for what Drago was called.

The moans grew louder and more frequent, making the hairs on his arms stand up and his trigger finger twitch. The anxiousness biting at his need to know had his leg shaking faster and his pulse hammering under his skin.

"Has the government labeled them?" Patience no longer resided within him. It had all seeped out. He knew damn well what Drago's ability, eating habits, and behavior was pointing towards him being, but he wanted Dana to say it already.

"I don't like to say the word the government uses, and I don't want to confirm that such creatures exist. They cast a reflection in mirrors. I've never seen fangs. I've never tested to see if they are allergic to garlic, and I have never taken the time to brandish a cross. I have this natural instinct to kill them. The mere sight of them sickens me, makes my blood boil in my veins, and I can hardly control my blood-lusting urge when I'm around them."

This was the second time she'd mentioned her intense urge to kill the creatures. Was she its mortal enemy in some way? Based on what he'd seen so far, she wasn't one-hundred percent human herself.

"And despite what you may think, they don't have a problem with daylight. Some of them are pale and some aren't. So far, the only way I can distinguish them from us is by their scent, their speed, and their weird attraction to me. They give off a spicy, ginger scent that is so strong, it's suffocating."

Neal took in her dark form while considering her words. The picture Dana was painting was revealing itself and it grew claws, fangs, and possessed an insatiable need to drink blood.

"Drago asked for your blood in exchange for killing a man. I agree with the government's label. What else could they be but vamp—"

"No! Don't say it," she cut him off. "Don't speak the word. The v-word was my first assumption. Given the weird, hard to explain, and paranormal shit that I've encountered, I refuse to breathe power into their existence because it will force me to ask a question I've been avoiding answering."

Her deep inhalation followed an exhausting exhale that filled the cabin, drowning out the moaning coming from the head.

"Why would a group of blood-sucking creatures be interested in killing my mother? Despite all I've seen and experienced, I'm naively holding out for science to explain them, and me, for that matter."

Another moan filled the car, and Neal hated the spine-gnawing sound.

"When you were recruited, did you receive the in-briefing about The Breeze, us, and the other dimensions, The Vault and The Hollow, and how every type of creature we were led to believe was a fairytale had the probability of being alive in one of the dimensions?"

"Yes," she answered quickly. "Most of it is hard to believe unless you see it, but *we* exist, so it's always in the back of my mind that *they* exist too. I'm always wondering about all that history on interlocking dimensions being the gateway to heaven and hell. If it's all true, death is truly the beginning of a long journey."

The amount of history Neal was given during his in-briefing with TOP had given him a splitting headache. Some of the information had the probability of being true, some he'd have to see to believe, and some he was convinced were unproven theories. Yet, here he was, riding around with a screaming vampire head.

"I didn't believe in that thing in the back of your car until I saw it. Therefore, I agree with you. It's hard to wrap your mind around something you can't see or prove. Unless I go to The Vault, or The Hollow, I can't say that they exist, but I can't say that they don't either."

The conversation died down, like it had been sucked into the blackhole of the unknown that surrounded them. Darkness was dumped over him like a bucket of ice water when Dana flipped off the headlights. It dawned on him that he was so engrossed in finding answers that he hadn't paid much attention to where they were headed.

Dana turned into an alley that led to a stretch of abandoned warehouses. She drove along the dark, tight alley with ease and no headlights. Speed may not have been the only ability she possessed. Their surroundings were entrenched in a thick, demanding darkness, so intense, he could hardly see his own hands inside the car. As oddly as it sounded in his head, the intensity of the darkness surrounding them gave him a strange sense of Déjà vu. He shivered from the chill that came out of nowhere and gripped him. Dana's voice sneaked up on him like she often did and rescued him from the strange vibes invading his internal space.

"In case you're wondering where we're going, this is where I take their heads to burn them. I was brought here by a target the government assigned me to track. He brought me here to eat me, dismember me, or burn my body. Since he was a homicidal maniac, he'd probably planned to do all three. He was one of *them*. Not one of the five that killed my mother, but one, nonetheless. Since I've dipped my toes into their world, I come in contact with them more often than I'd like."

He sensed her eyes on him, assessing his reaction.

"The incinerator still works in one of these old warehouses. When he brought me here, he had no idea I was as fast as him. I managed to get him wedged between two beams and commenced to chopping off his head. I tossed the head in the fire, and he instantly yelled the walls off the building and spilled his guts. In an effort to stop me from burning his head fully, he divulged valuable secrets about them. Detaching specific body parts is the key to killing them, or permanently hurting them."

Good to know, Neal thought.

"I started using this place to get rid of them since my target no longer needs it. I listened to his screams and watched his head burn until there was nothing but ash left. Once his head was destroyed, I was set to burn the rest of him, but without the head, his body turned into a puddle of blood."

Was it wrong for him to have a smile inching across his lips? The beautiful, diplomatic princess was a stone-cold killer. How she managed to keep the details of her deadly life from seeping into her normal, prim and proper one was impressive.

This was why she snuck away and valued her alone time. A large part of her life was filled with monsters, and she'd had to become one to prevent them from consuming her.

"When you were shot by the cops in that truck, did it have something to do with these things?" he asked, hoping to get more of his curiosity satisfied.

"It was them. Apparently, the last one I need to track down is some type of a leader. I got too close to finding him. A group of them ganged up on me and almost succeeded in killing me by setting up that truck scene. They are clever in staying hidden and good at avoiding anything that leads to them being discovered."

A flicker of intrigue gripped Neal, but he didn't know why the agency would choose now to introduce him to this aspect of their underworld. They wanted him here with Dana, and he knew they would never give him a straightforward answer as to why.

CHAPTER SIXTEEN

DANA

DANA DROVE through a huge hole she had discovered in the side wall of the old, abandoned warehouse she'd adopted as her own personal slaughterhouse. She was aware her actions had Neal on edge, but he was keeping secrets too. He had promptly deflected her question about his ability, but she hadn't forgotten. It was a question she would revisit.

She drove far enough into the dark building to avoid being seen by the lonely guard who drove past every two hours, patrolling the area. When she opened her car door, the automatic interior lights provided enough illumination for her to see Neal's roaming gaze as he searched the dark interior of the building.

"You can get out, if you want," she announced.

Dana reached blindly into the back of her car and retrieved a lantern. The bright beams easily cut through the thick darkness, making the area around her car spring to life. Neal exited the car, taking careful strides. He kept his weapon at the ready, and she didn't blame him.

Based on Neal's reaction to the creatures she'd been hunting her whole career, it appeared the agency assigned them cases that coincided with the type of abilities they possessed. If that were true and her ability contended with the types of monsters she hunted, then what type of ability was Neal hiding?

He'd mentioned rescue missions, hunting down *rixies* that could disrupt time and manifest enough force to kill humans. Neal was being tightlipped about what he hunted for the agency because he didn't want her piecing together any more than he wanted her to know right now. The kinds of things he hunted and the type of missions he'd told her he was assigned didn't give any definitive clues of where Neal fell on the supernatural spectrum. There was still the mystery of how he'd been able to follow her to the bridge, post up, and not be detected.

After opening the trunk, she cracked the chest open and cast a stern glance inside at Drago's head. "Don't you dare bite me." She pointed a stiff finger like she was chastising a hardheaded child. "If you do, I'll make you suffer," she promised.

When she opened the chest fully, Drago's burning red eyes darted up angrily. Neal aimed his weapon at the head.

"Return me to my body, and I'll give you the last one," Drago shouted.

Drago's words gave Dana pause. It had taken her years of broken bones, bruises and scrapes, chasing ghosts, killing and re-killing monsters, and still, she had never seen the face of the main one. The idea that she could find him faster tempted her.

She snatched Drago's head from the chest. "I don't believe you. You were ready to kill me on that bridge. Why? Does your leader know that I'm hunting him? Did I get too close? Did he order you to kill me? What is his name?"

The questions were fired off so fast, it would be a miracle if he understood even one of them.

The leader had taken the biggest bite from her mother. When things became chaotic, he snapped her mother's neck. The others contributed, yes, but the one that caused her mother's death was the one Dana wanted the most and had never found.

His name was a mystery, but she remembered the tattoo on his wrist—an octagonal shaped crest, outlined in black, with hieroglyphic symbols she didn't understand. Seeing that crest all those years ago had helped her track the others.

Drago wore his crest as a neck tattoo. The first two monsters she'd killed wore theirs on their wrists, like their leader. Since they all bore the mark, Dana had discovered that their kind marked each other in that manner because the symbol represented their clan or family crest. It was too bad there weren't any databases dedicated to monster markings and symbols that could have provided her a least an origin point for the group. Many of the systems and guidelines they needed to be more effective agents were still in the production phases since work in the supernatural field was relatively new.

A toe-curling scream that creased her face in anger spilled from Drago's mouth.

"What the hell is your problem? I haven't touched you yet."

He took harsh breaths which made her question, briefly, the intricacies of his oxygen flow since his lungs were two counties away from his head.

"They are moving my body. I can feel it. I have been around for one hundred sixty years, and this is the freakiest, scariest shit I've ever experienced."

"I don't give a damn about your discomfort, Drago. Enough with the theatrics. Answer my questions before I start lighting your face on fire. And I'll take my time burning you until there is nothing left."

The statement got him talking again. "His name is Linkin. No one knows where he lives. We only know his face. He meets with us on his own terms."

Dana shook her head, her lips pinched in irritation. "Let me ask you something, Drago. How much do you value your life?

Do you have a strong will to live when your life is in jeopardy, or do you not care since you likely don't have a soul?"

Neal stood about ten feet away, observing.

"I'm telling you what I know." Drago's voice went up a few octaves, and the flicker of the cigarette lighter in her hand made his eyes grow as wide as silver dollars. Neal leaned in their direction, his eyes riveted to the action.

"I don't know where he lives. He's never revealed it to any of us. Please! Don't!"

The idea of making Drago suffer pleased Dana. As far as she was concerned, he'd admitted to killing people for over a century and a half, feasting on human flesh and blood. The flame licked his cheek, forcing him to release a shriek loud enough to wake the dead. Since his head wasn't attached to his body, his wounds wouldn't heal.

"Start talking or you're going to need a good witch doctor to fix your face."

The fire continued to eat at his cheek until the stench of burning flesh found its way up her nose.

Neal fanned a hand in front of his scrunched nose. "Damn, that reeks."

"He owns the Harrington Building! Stop. Please, stop!" came Drago's shrill cries.

Dana let the flame die. She knew of the building. It housed apartments, offices, businesses, and a few restaurants and boutiques on the bottom level. She didn't have a reason to visit, but the Gourmet Symphony restaurant inside it was popular, even among her employees.

"Keep talking. This is a new lighter, and I also have an incinerator at my disposal."

"A friend of mine, Brandon, works for Linkin, but like I told you earlier, we never see him."

Dana wasn't as concerned about the leader's looks as she was in knowing where to find him. The sound of his voice would never be forgotten. The crest tattooed on his skin would also be enough to identify him, right before she chopped off his head.

"What's his full name?" She flicked the lighter. "If your friend works for him, there should be a name on his business documents, shouldn't it?"

Drago's face twitched, and she wasn't sure if it was in pain or anger. "He uses the name Linkin Kellerman for business and when associating with people. That's all I know."

"No. That's not all you know. The crest on your neck says you're from the same clan, or you're possibly a family member. You need to spill some god-damned beans, or I'll spill whatever your brain is made of. I'll open your skull, scoop out parts of your brain, and make you watch me burn it."

Drago was the so-called monster, but after those words, his wide unblinking gaze never left hers.

"Does he live in the building? Is he ever at his building or any of the businesses inside?"

Drago took too long to respond, so she flicked the lighter a few more times.

"I have never seen him there, but he owns the building and likely makes appearances from time to time."

Dana continued to torture Drago until the sound of his voice made her physically ill. Once she believed she'd had as much as she would get from him, this round, she muzzled and returned his mutilated head to the chest.

She and Neal had been out all night and a few hours of sleep would be all they would get before they were due to go into the office and start the *normal* workday.

CHAPTER SEVENTEEN

DANA

WHEN DANA CREPT through the window she left cracked, the dimly lit house accepted her with welcoming warmth. Her car along with Drago's head and the body that TOP would collect was parked at a small underground bunker she'd secretly built outside the property.

She gleamed past one of the security guards so fast, the wind from her passage ruffled his hair. By the time she made it to her bedroom door, Neal was standing there, smiling.

The questions in her mind must have been expressed in her gaze. She had left Neal outside and foolishly assumed he was searching for a way across the fence and past the security guards. Instead, he had beat her into the house.

"I want a full explanation. Secrets, remember? We aren't keeping them anymore," she told him.

A *swish* ruffled her hair, followed by a muffled *pop* that made her jump. Her left hand covered her chest and her right went over her mouth to keep Neal from seeing how wide his actions left her mouth hanging open. She stifled a scream, lest she have every guard on the property coming to check her status.

Neal had disappeared before her eyes and reemerged, across

the hall at his bedroom door. She nearly jumped out of her skin when he phased out of sight and flashed right back in front of her.

He turned his hands up and shrugged nonchalantly at her response. "Figured it would be easier to show you because I can't explain how it works. It was how I was able to follow you. I don't know what it is that makes it happen, nor do I know what it's called. All I know is, if I can see and have an accurate idea of where I will end up, I can send myself there. Based on what I studied in TOP's supernatural history library, I'm labeled a *Bendy*. There are many accounts and studies dedicated to attempting to explain what happens while I'm jumping. I don't know if I'm jumping through time, or if I'm phasing in and out of space, or if my molecules are breaking down at a rapid rate of speed and moving faster than light."

Stuck in silence, Dana swallowed hard. Her stare remained unblinking and her lips refused to close.

"You're the only person who's seen me do this up close and personal. I've always been afraid to show anyone, even other agents. Honestly, the first time it happened, I thought I had a mental disorder that allowed me to convince myself that I possessed this ability. It wasn't until I saw other agents in the field use their abilities that I believed in my own. When I saw the way you and Drago moved on the bridge, and after all you have revealed to me tonight, I feel like I can breathe easier than I ever have before."

Captivated, Dana didn't know what question to ask first. Although it was evident that all TOP agents possessed something extra, she had never seen anyone else do what Neal was capable of doing. Her area of expertise had always been targeted at the creatures she hunted.

"What does it feel like when it happens? Can you still see? Think? Why..." She jumped from one question to the next, not giving him time to answer the first.

Neal chuckled. "This is the first time I've seen you flustered. Why don't we get ready for work? I'll explain it as best I can on the drive to the office."

Her hands were up to his chest level and closing in for a hug. The radiating heat wafting off of him warmed her fingertips and tempted her closer. The action stopped when she managed to drop her arms. After all the secrets they had revealed to each other, she felt closer to him, connected by an unbreakable thread. Only he had gotten an in depth peek into her true identity.

She took a quick shower, anxious to get back to Neal so he could fill her in on his amazing ability. Now that their secrets were being laid out on the table, the crushing weight of the world didn't push down on her shoulders as hard.

A knock sounded at her door as she was pinning her hair up. She swung her door open with bobby pins poking from her mouth, like a bunch of metal buck teeth.

"Come in," she called, her words muffled. She wore her hair up so much she could pin it into any number of elaborate or simple buns.

Neal stepped inside while she pushed in the last few hair pins.

After closing the door, she turned the lock and stood facing the hard wood before turning to face Neal. What she was about to do was scandalous, but Neal had to know by now that she was attracted to him.

She dropped her black silk robe, revealing a nude-colored bra and panty set, so sheer, you could literally see everything.

Neal stood at the foot of her bed, awaiting her next move with smiling excitement resting on his lips. The intense hunger that surfaced in his eyes turned her passion into gas and her desire into fire.

She turned in each direction, giving him a view from multiple angles. Initially, she assumed he might disapprove of her behavior, but he had decided to keep a pair of her panties and sat in her office and watched her with lust-heavy eyes while he'd sniffed them.

Their little office foreplay session had raised her blood pressure to its max, and Dana was finally giving it the response she believed it deserved. Lazy steps brought her closer to him, their gazes locked.

"Neal," she called, letting a seductive purr drip from her tone.

His face gave away nothing, but his eyes conveyed a well-versed story of longing and desire.

"Yes?"

Another lingering step drew her closer. "I don't think I'm going to make it to work today."

"Why not?" he asked, managing to keep his face devoid of emotion.

He knew damn well why she wasn't going to make it, and it was his fault.

She fondled her breast, her fingers meandering along the curves of her body. "I'm warm to the touch. My blood pressure is elevated. My breathing is a bit erratic. I need you to alleviate this pressure and help me regain control of these strong urges I can't shake. Will you do that for me, Neal?"

His teeth bit into a sexy smile. "I'm here to see you through all of your problems. What do you need me to do?"

She swore the rays pinging off her smile brightened the interior of her room. Dana took the final step. Without her heels, Neal towered above her. The soft hair at her hairline flirted with the short stubble on his chin. She favored heels because she hated being looked down on by anyone. A fresh pair of heels always seemed to put a little extra spark in her confidence as well. However, Neal's downcast gaze sent jolts of erotic impulses all over her body. Maybe it was the lust in his eyes; she didn't know and didn't have time to think on it too much. He'd asked her what she needed him to do, and he deserved an answer.

"I need you to alleviate my suffering."

What she didn't tell him was that she suffered from sexual starvation. Finding a man who could handle her sexual appetite was a daunting task, and she hoped Neal was up for the challenge because she was so turned on she planned to fuck him until his soul begged for her to have mercy.

Dana could no longer restrain herself. Whatever he was about to say was lost between his lips and hers. She used her speed to sling her arms around his neck and yanked him closer so that their lips were nearly touching. The action left his lips parted in surprise. She reminded herself to move at a normal person's speed, no matter how much *Sevyn*, her alter ego, wanted to hurry things along.

Speed was never her friend when it came to sex, so Dana did her best to calm her raging hormones. Her kisses became tender presses and in return, she was rewarded by the skin-tingling caresses of Neal's soft lips.

The man made excellent use of his lips and tongue, producing slow, sensual kisses that felt like he was making love to her mouth. Breathy moans bubbled up from her throat, interrupting the breaths of air she'd fought to inhale.

When she finally unhinged her arms from around his neck, a hint of hesitation found its way into the corners of his mouth and the edges of his eyes.

"Are you sure?"

Neal asked the question, but it didn't stop him from sliding fingers, feather light, across her nipple. And he was the one who'd claimed she was putting on a performance. She didn't reply but used speed to grip his hands and slide them over the globes of her ass until he cupped her plump cheeks.

"Did you really ask me that silly question? This is all I could think about after you put your hands up my skirt. You have no idea how badly you made me want you. If my assistant hadn't come to the door when she did, *this* probably would have happened back *then.*"

They didn't waste any more words. Dana relieved Neal of his clothes, admiring his strong male frame which was toned and produced enough definition to fill up a dictionary. She took his pants but not his boxers, purposefully keeping herself in suspense. The large bulge that pressed against the thin material had her yearning to see what he was hiding.

Her hand skimmed his solid chest, his toned abs, and finally made the journey to his waistband. Neal stood, perfectly content with letting her explore whatever piqued her interest. She liked that he didn't hesitate to stroke and caress whatever part on her body called his attention.

Her thumbs slid into the waistband of his boxers and she shoved them down until the trunk of his dick stopped them. She continued, taking great care in sliding the boxers past the area growing bigger before her eyes.

His hard flesh surfaced, urging her to inch the material down further. Her gradual pace made the material glide along his hard, peachy flesh like she was peeling back a layer from a ripe banana.

This wasn't fruit. He was *all* male.

When a good six inches was unveiled and more remained hidden, it took everything to contain the rush of excitement coursing through her. When he was fully revealed, her lips drifted apart and she stood, staring, like she had never seen a dick before. It wasn't that she'd never seen one, but she hadn't seen one like Neal's.

At first, the sight of him surprised her until the corners of her mouth gradually raised into a smile. Her tongue slid across her lips as her mind worked overtime plotting out sex scenes before he'd even touched her. The possibilities with him were endless. She admired the impressive expanse of his dick a few moments longer to banish any ideas that she was imagining it. She forced her eyes to meet his unreadable gaze.

"It looks like I've found another of your big secrets."

The statement put a smirk on his face.

"Is that so?"

Her hand gravitated towards that tempting jewel and with the first caress, she released a long-winded sigh, imagining what it would be like to have him inside her. Fondling him, her fantasy played out while she stroked from the base to the head and found it difficult to tear her eyes away to see if her touch pleased him.

She delighted in the sound of the low groans that escaped his throat, the slight sway in his body, and the sight of his half-lidded eyes. His accelerated breaths tickled her skin, causing a warm tingled to dance across the surface. She hadn't decided yet if she was more fascinated with his dick or his amazing ability to transport from one place to the next.

Reluctantly, she let go of her new fascination and sent his boxers the rest of the way down his legs. A temporary lapse in discipline allowed her need for speed to take control. She stripped out of her underwear in a flash before she and Neal went speeding into the bed from her energetic shove.

The mattress groaned under their crashing weight, and they bounced upwards, a few times, before settling into the cushiness of the bed.

Their temporary laughter gave way to unrelenting lust.

Her lips pressed into his with an assured firmness that lured his tongue between her sultry lips and into her mouth. Neal never let his hands leave her body since it begged with shuddering heat for his smooth, electrifying touch.

She bent, straddling him as he sat up, moving in tandem with her. Her eyes locked with his, connecting to the intensity in his dreamy stare which scared her as much as it excited her.

Eye contact was broken when she reached towards her

bedside table. Unwilling to break her connection with his warm body, she stretched to open the drawer to retrieve a sleeve of twelve condoms. Thankfully, she'd purchased a variety of sizes.

She assumed, once again, that her brazen behavior would surprise him, but she easily interpreted the C's Neal possessed—charisma and confidence. He didn't care that she was bold or shameless.

"If we can manage it, I would like to use every one of these before we leave this room."

He leaned in and gave her a playful peck on the lips. "I'll do whatever it takes to make it happen."

His dick jumped under her thigh to add spice to his words. She knew they couldn't physically use all those condoms, but she was damn well going to try. The knowledge that he was willing to go along with her and having seen and touched what he had to offer, made the escapade that much more appealing.

She tore off one of the condoms, her eyes straying to the big hard prize cradled between their bodies. He sprang free, hard, and ready when she scooted back. The sight of him, thick and plump with a pearl of precum seeping from the tip, had her tongue darting out of her mouth to lick her lips.

"May I?"

He tightened the grip he had on her thighs, keeping his lust-heavy eyes on hers.

"I'm all yours."

Did he have any idea he was like a big, tasty package of drugs, telling an addict to take what she wanted? She presented prim and proper to her family and associates, but in the bedroom, she didn't like to limit herself.

Her eyes remained on his as she clinched the condom wrapper between her teeth and tore the edge, pulling it with her thumb and forefinger. Her anxious hand wrapped firmly around him at the base while she rolled the condom on with the other, enjoying the hard and silky feel. The sight of what sat in the palm of her hand made her lady parts pulse with eagerness.

"I'll give you foreplay later. Right now, I can't wait to get you inside me."

Condom in place, she kept her hand firmly wrapped around him while raising herself higher on her knees. Neal took advantage of her breast passing so teasingly close to his face, letting his tongue graze the hard, dark tips of her nipples. Her teeth gritted from the effort she exerted in an attempt to keep things at a normal pace.

She hovered above the tip of him before she eased down, her tight wet heat welcoming him. A mixture of a sigh and a moan escaped with the first few inches she took. The gripping sensation of the warm, wet slide had Neal balling his fist and squeezing his eyes shut so tight, his head shook involuntarily.

Slowly, Dana, she reminded herself. *Don't rush it.*

A bit more was eased in and the firm pressure of his throbbing hardness plunging into her held promises of overloading her senses. She waved her body, working him in as leisurely as her brain would allow.

"Jesus, you feel good."

His words rushed out on one long breath. She draped her arms around his neck while her body kept to the slow tempo of their dance.

Savoring every splendid second, she leaned her forehead against his. Though she gave it a try, she failed to keep her fluttering eyes open. The rhythm of her movements sent addictive waves of pleasure deep into her, making her eyes roll to the back of her head. The waves vibrated outward until they spread all over her body and covered her in maddening heat. She lifted her head and kissed Neal, pressing her lips firmly into his before seeking out his tongue.

He let her devour him, and she took advantage of his giving nature. She was plunged into a world of pleasure, so compulsively addictive she welcomed losing herself in the sensation. Sheathing every enticing inch of him was a feat she thought impossible. However, her ravenous state had proven her wrong, and she fed on his sexual energy as well as his hard as steel member that filled her to capacity. Her lips raked his ear.

"Let's switch. I don't know how much longer I can control myself."

Neal drew Dana firmly into him, sending himself in even deeper.

"Oh!" His action made her call to the ceiling, and her body pulsed with electrifying currents of pleasure.

His hands rode the swirl of her rolling hips while he lavished her neck with light flicks of his lips and tongue. His warm breaths teased her ear, the puffs of air stroking a different level of desire.

"You don't have to control yourself with me. Do whatever you want."

Dana's head shook like that of an addict trying desperately to kick a long, ongoing habit. "I know when I can't do something and, right now, I'm losing control. I want us both to enjoy this. You have no idea how much discipline it's taking not to...not to..."

His throbbing hardness stole her breath once more as he pulsed inside her.

Neal's words blew out between ragged breaths against her trembling lips. "I'm not altogether sure I can control myself, either. You already have me on the verge of losing my mind. But, for you, I'll do my best."

Without another word, he flipped her, keeping their connection in place. Neal was planted so comfortably between Dana's legs; it was like he was right where he belonged. His first few strokes took her breaths and didn't give them back. His continued plunges took what was left of her mind and left her mouth open in an exaggerated O.

"Oh. God. Neal."

The man made love like nobody's business. If she had known this, she would have let him start this session. Dana made a confession she would never have made under any other circumstances.

"I take back what I said about you not being able to handle what's under my surface."

Neal smiled, but it was stolen by a wave of pleasure that left him gasping.

"You're devouring me, Dana. Shit!"

Wrapping his anxious fingers around her inner thighs, he lifted and positioned them so that the move tilted her pelvic area up and sent him impossibly deep. Harsh gasps had her nearly hyperventilating. At this point, he had her all pants and unintelligible cries. He kept a firm grasp of her thighs as he worked her body with the precision of a master love maker. She was dying and pleasure was the taker of her soul. He wasn't even moving fast, yet he had her body on fire.

"Am I alleviating your suffering?" His lusty question flowed into her ears like an invisible layer of spiked desire.

"Oh, God. Yes."

She couldn't have strung together a full sentence if her life depended on it. Neal didn't know it yet, but there was no damn way she was letting him end this affair. They hadn't finished their first round, but he had opened a door she wasn't going to let him shut.

"'Bout to. 'Bout to. Co-co-co..." Incomplete words was all she could manage before her body shattered and she came undone, soaked in every pleasure-filled moment.

Neal followed suit, the pleasure taking possession of his body with a series of quick spasms. His cries registered, but Dana's ears were too clogged with flowing pleasure as it crawled up and down her body, lingering on the surface before sinking deep into the core of her.

After what felt like hours, she fluttered back to the real world. Neal was giving her the one thing she'd been craving for years—satisfaction. The orgasm was so mind-blowingly good, the aftershocks continued flowing through her, lavishing her body with sporadic jolts of pleasure. Dana accepted, then and there, that she wasn't too proud to stalk Neal to get more. A lot more.

CHAPTER EIGHTEEN

NEAL

THE DELICATE SLIDE of fingers coaxed Neal's awakening. Manicured nails traced along his abs and traveled to the portion of him barely covered by the sheet. His gaze made its way up and found curious brown eyes, staring at him.

"Hey, beautiful."

There was no mistaking the lustful glint in her eyes, the glide of her tongue across her lips, and the placement of her hand on his dick.

Her hungry eyes trapped his. "Can I have some more, please?"

He didn't know where she'd dragged them from, but the sleeve of condoms was back.

A huge smile danced across his face. "You can have as much as you want. Besides, I love alleviating your suffering."

Accompanying his words, his dick waved in her hand, like it was a part of the conversation. Dana wanted more, and more was what he was about to give her.

Neal didn't know how long they'd been asleep this time, but the position of the sun through the thin drapes indicated it was at least noon. He vaguely remembered a guard knocking on the door. Dana had thrown on his T-shirt to greet the guard before he could spring the door open, informing him that she was sick and taking the day off. Neal had passed out since but knew the guard would eventually return because it was their job to have eyes on Dana.

He shook his head, attempting to ward off Dana's mesmerizing effect on him. Her body was a beacon that zeroed in on his senses and had him running a hand up her thigh before letting it travel along her stomach. He cupped a perfect breast, which were an exact fit to his palm with their small raisin-sized hard nipples. Her skin, soft with her alluring bronzed tint left you switching back and forth between what color you were actually looking at, brown or deep caramel. She stirred, her smile greeting him before her eyes fluttered open.

Three condoms were missing from the sleeve now. He had never tested his stamina like this and was learning that with Dana, it wasn't hard to summon the strength. His will to please her was as strong as the extreme amounts of desire she stirred within him each time she expressed she wanted him.

Although she made his desire soar, there was a question he'd been dying to ask her. He brushed aside a lock of hair that had fallen from her bun. Surprisingly, the bun remained intact after all the thrusting and moving they'd been engaged in. He sat up, bringing her up with him and assisted her across his thighs, loving their closeness.

"Why don't you ever wear your hair down?"

Dana stopped the tender pecks she was placing on his chin and neck like he had doused her with freezing water. Her eyes remained on his chest longer than he liked, so Neal placed a finger under her chin and made her look into his eyes.

"What's the matter? Is something wrong with your hair? I

feel like I can tell you anything, and I hope that you feel the same."

She remained silent with her eyes pinned on his for an odd moment before she began removing bobby pins from her hair. Neal counted ten hairpins, so far, and the bun still hadn't fallen.

"This is going to sound crazy, but my hair has something to do with why the monsters I hunt are drawn to me. When I wear it down, they are more fascinated, stunned even."

Although he hadn't intended it to, his laugh sneaked out. "Dana, you're a beautiful woman. I don't think you need your hair down for men to fall all over themselves. Sometimes you're oblivious to how men react to you. Since it is my job to watch you, I've seen the stares, the lurking eyes, and men tripping all over themselves. It's not just monsters you're attracting."

She didn't appear convinced.

"My hair makes me different. I can't explain it, but I can show you."

She untwisted her bun and long tresses of hair fell past her shoulders and cascaded down her body like a dark, curly curtain. Now he understood why she needed all the hair pins. Her hair was thick, wavy, and long enough to stretch past her chest and fall over her breasts like strings of black silk. She was in profile, so he couldn't see her face while she shook the last remaining coils loose.

When she turned and faced him, his smile dropped and his ability to move and form words switched off. There was an energetic radiance that projected from her. The energy possessed the power to strangle his vocal cords while holding his gaze prisoner.

The oxygen flowing to Neal's lungs stalled. His lips moved in preparation to release words, but each syllable floated away on a lost breath, unspoken. His roaming eyes drank her in with an addicting intensity he'd never before experienced. The sight of her had taken ownership of his senses, leaving him only the will to sit there and stare.

"Neal? You're staring at me like I stare at the monsters when I can't fight off the urge to kill them."

He cleared his throat but was unable to shake the effect of seeing her this way. She raised her hands, took up each side of her hair, and shoved it back.

Neal stopped her, placing a delicate hand over hers. "Wait. Let me look at you for a bit longer."

She remained in place, and he was grateful for the extra time. The sight of her gave him a fulfilling sense of bliss he'd never experienced before. He'd seen others affected this way by agents who had the ability to hypnotize people.

Dana hadn't accepted yet that she didn't need her hair to possess people. This influence she had over one's senses was a part of her, like her speed. She turned away from him and began the process of pinning her hair back.

Neal shook off the effect, shutting his eyes tight to clear his mind enough to think straight. She had taken his voice and his concentration so swiftly; he hadn't been able to summon the parts of his brain that would allow him to regain his motor functions. He was still recovering from the haze of the blissful possession while she braided her hair in one long plait.

Was it embarrassment he saw flash in her gaze when she finally lifted her eyes?

"That's why I don't wear my hair down. It's why I wear a wig when I'm working. I don't know what it is about my hair that makes me so different, but it makes some normal men more aggressive and reckless, and it does strange things to the monsters."

She saw it as a nuisance, but he saw it for what it was. Another ability.

"I never know what it will make the monsters do. It took me years to figure out why some men couldn't seem to help treating me like a piece of fresh meat, and it took me becoming a coldhearted bitch to figure out that it has something to do with me not being one-hundred percent human. Sometimes, it works in my favor, giving me an advantage over the monsters. Sometimes, it makes them crazy enough to try to take a bite out of me. You, it makes speechless."

Neal drew in a deep breath, his chest rising high before falling.

"I believe you're what I've heard other agents refer to as *hyphenated*, meaning you have more than one ability. Have you ever considered that your hair is as much an ability as your speed?"

Although he didn't admit it, he hadn't fully shaken off the effect.

"No," she answered, her brows drawn tight and her gaze searching his face as she considered his suggestion.

"You have the ability to sway humans and supernatural beings. It's likely something you can do without letting your hair down, but you've never seen it as a gift or an ability, so you've adapted your hair as the key to triggering it."

She swallowed hard. "I've never considered it an ability. I still have trouble trying to figure out the genetic code on how I ended up this way with human parents. So, what did you see that is so different than when I have my hair up versus down?"

The question evoked a smile at the memory of the vision she had presented.

"It's like seeing the most beautiful thing in the world that you want to marvel at, and take in, because your mind is convincing you that you may never get a chance to see it again, and the last thing you want is to forget it."

Her eyebrows lifted but she didn't comment.

"Looking at you with your hair down is like that, but to the tenth power. It's like a natural stimulant that heightens my dopamine levels. If I'd been someone you were tracking, you could have easily taken me out by simply letting your hair down."

She flashed a little twisted smirk. "I think you may have just helped me discover another weapon to add to my arsenal."

Another long pause followed her comment and Neal sensed a change based on her hard stare. She was ready to turn the spotlight on him.

"You have another secret too." Her knowing smirk deepened.

He didn't reply right away, wasn't sure how.

"Neal, sometimes I see this deep sadness behind your eyes that you attempt to hide, but I see things faster than the average person, remember?"

His forced smile surfaced, barely bending his thinly stretched lips.

"It's not a secret you see. My history falls more along the lines of a mystery."

Her confused expression was enough for him to continue.

"Seven years ago, I was diagnosed with amnesia. The best doctors they could find couldn't even diagnose what kind of amnesia I have because I'm missing nineteen years."

Her eyes widened as utter disbelief flashed across her face. "Wait, did you say nineteen years? You're twenty-six. What am I missing?"

"I was essentially born at nineteen. At least, that was when I discovered myself. I was found at the top of the Anderson Building in DC. I don't even know how I ended up on the roof of one of the tallest buildings in the city. When I cracked my eyes open, I was staring into the twin faces of two businessmen, Drake and Damon Anderson, and Drake's wife. The brothers are the reason I was introduced to the agency. They own a multi-million-dollar company, but secretly worked for TOP.

"I was with the brothers and their doctor for about a week before I was transferred to a TOP medical facility. For months, they monitored me and ran numerous tests, trying to figure out what had caused my amnesia, but they never found an answer. I couldn't recall where I'd come from or who I was. My first and only memories started at the top of that building. Whenever I have downtime, I use all the resources the agency offers to look into a past I can't remember, but I have yet to find anything. No one is searching for me or has reported me missing. I didn't have any warrants or a criminal background. My fingerprints weren't in any databases. It was like I just, appeared."

Her pitying expression vanished in a flash and was quickly replaced with an unreadable one.

"Doctors estimated that I was at least nineteen, and all I came into this world with is this scar."

Neal could see all sorts of wheels turning in Dana's head.

"So, you have no recollection of your childhood? Nothing at all? Wait, how did you learn everything so quickly? Technically, you're seven, but you don't appear to be at a disadvantage."

He shrugged. "I remembered nothing, but my body possessed muscle memory of things that I must have done in the past. I never know the extent of what I know, even now, until I'm put in a situation to react. I'm not at a disadvantage because I was born, or reborn, with my factory settings. I knew how to read, write, communicate, and learn.

"It was determined that I either had some tactical training before I was found or possessed the capacity to learn quickly. The fact that I was never locked down or made to feel like a prisoner made me trust the agency. They taught, and I learned. It was like I'd been groomed specifically for the program. They even suggested that I may have been a member of a similar group and my memories were wiped so that I couldn't give up secrets. The weirdest thing about my situation is that every test they ran on me says that there's nothing physically wrong that would obstruct my memories. It's like someone or something literally stole them from me."

Dana hugged him long and hard, her arms shaking from the

strength she poured into the caress. "I know you don't want my pity, but I can't help being sympathetic to what you must feel. What if, within those nineteen years, there are things that are so horrible that it's a good thing you don't have your memories?"

"I've thought about that, and it's what keeps me from obsessing about my situation."

Neal wanted many things from Dana, but her feeling sorry for him wasn't one of them. He had come to terms with his situation a long time ago, but it wasn't until he'd made first contact with Dana that he believed the flashes he started seeing lately were memories. The castle-like stone house, the city of fire and screaming people, the endless living darkness.

Neal often skirted the subject of talking about himself. He had no idea what he'd been seeing in his head or dreaming about lately. There was always a heavy unease afterwards that made him want to flush his mind of every thought.

A slow smile crept across his lips at the sight of Dana, his perfect distraction and the only person to ever make him feel like he wasn't missing anything.

"I want you to sit on my face."

DANA

Those words sent Dana's senses soaring, and the sorrow she'd felt for Neal was burned away by the heat of passion he'd swept up in her. She stood to take off his T-shirt, but he stopped her by gripping her around her waist.

"Don't take anything off. I have to taste you, right now."

Shit!

The statement gave her a spark of energy that caused her to put some pep in her movement. Once she climbed over him, he gripped her hips, and she was swooped up to his face like she had climbed aboard a carnival ride. She didn't know how he unwrapped her so fast, but he managed to slip her panties to the side with one hand and his other was wrapped around one of her ass cheeks.

While her pulsing wet core slid against his strong, waving tongue, she closed her eyes to sensations that had her gasping for air and praying that the pleasuring enlightenment he was bestowing on her never stopped.

Lustful cries that sounded like they were traveling a great distance spilled free. His tongue was hot and firm, and the hypnotic qualities of it had her mind floating and her body draped in pleasure. Her attempts to breathe were sabotaged each time he twirled his tongue around her clit. His expert actions gave her mini orgasms that stole her voice but didn't stop her from expressing her pleasure through her body language.

Each word she struggled to say was being stolen, snatched up and tucked into the folds of her desire. Neal lifted her to adjust her body's weight. When he had her where he wanted, he let her weight rest on his face and mouth. He deliberately buried himself in her pulsing flesh and hot juices, and his moans confirmed he enjoyed this scene as much as she did.

Knock. Knock.

They froze. Why hadn't she relocked her door after the last security check? No sooner had she thought it, her door creaked open.

Howard, one of the guards, peeked in through the crack he'd opened. Too stunned to move, Dana sat there on Neal's face, caught in the act. She stretched the shirt he had insisted she keep on to cover his head, while staring at the guard like she wasn't getting freaky with the man who was supposed to be protecting her.

"Hey, Miss Diallo, I'm checking to make sure you're okay. I was doing my normal rounds, and thought I heard yelling."

Howard didn't appear surprised by their display, which had her taking quick glances over her shoulder

At the angle she and Neal were in, it was possible Howard hadn't noticed Neal under her, yet. His body lay flat and with her covering his head, it gave him the right amount of conceal-ment to keep him hidden in plain sight.

Howard tilted his head and wrinkled his brows, eyeing her suspiciously. "Miss Diallo, what…what're you doing?"

She sat in an elevated kneeling position with her legs spread. One hand gripped the edge of her mattress while the other fought to hold the shirt over Neal's head. She didn't have control of her winded breathing, either. How could she? Neal's tongue was still buried inside her.

She said the first thing that came to mind. "I'm okay. I was meditating and trying to relax my mind."

Based on his pinched lips, Howard didn't believe her ridicu-lous lie one bit. His face wrinkled tighter in confusion. The possibility that he was oblivious to what was actually happening became stronger by the second. He hadn't noticed Neal yet, and Neal must have figured as much because he hadn't moved an inch. She glanced back once more at her tousled bedding and the thrown about pillows that helped to conceal the scandalous situation.

Howard inclined his head. "You have a good evening, Miss Diallo."

The creases of his face gave away his attempt to figure out her actions. She flashed a smile, continuing to hold her odd position.

"Howard, will you do me a favor before you go?"

"Sure."

"Will you lock my door for me?"

He turned his body further into the room, his attention focused on his task at hand. He reached around and pushed in her lock from the inside. His cheeks had flushed, a blushing pink surfacing on them. He was too embarrassed to glance in her direction now that he thought he knew what she was doing to *herself*.

Once the door was closed, Dana let out a ragged breath, only to have Neal steal it away. Once he knew the coast was clear, he continued where he'd left off, his tongue burrowing deep enough to send instant shots of pleasure sailing through her body.

It hadn't taken but a few intoxicating flicks of his tongue to make her forget the predicament they had just been caught in and had somewhat escaped.

CHAPTER NINETEEN

SEVYN

As MUCH AS Dana wanted to stay snuggled up to Neal, she had work to do. The need to check out Drago's lead called to her addiction.

We're out here. Come and hunt us.

This was the chant she heard echoing inside her head every time the urge to hunt hit her.

She didn't want to drag Neal into her world of madness again so soon. It was why she was sneaking away from him at one in the morning.

They had managed to use six of the twelve condoms in less than a twenty-four hour period. She never expected that Neal would go along with her crazy request to use all twelve, but she loved that he was willing to accept the challenge. Early on, she had gotten the impression that he wasn't one to give up on anything easily. He'd not only given her the best sex of her life, but he managed to do it, repeatedly.

However, it was time to set aside her romantic fantasies and suit up.

She jumped into the sleek, new black tactical suit that TOP had issued for testing. It was made from bulletproof material, had built-in night vision, and a few other features that would come in handy for her kind of work.

The long sleeves were fitted with a thin metal ring that could be used for striking an adversary or detaching to become circular blades. The suit was also flame retardant, shock absorbing, and had built-in chest and back protection. Best of all, it was strong enough to stand up to a close-range shotgun blast.

She added a bit of her own special design to the suit, that included slots to strap on her favorite long blades, or swords, as some might call them. Tonight she decided to carry just one, Queen, since Drago's lead hadn't sounded promising.

Admiring the blade, she ran her nail across the serrated portion close to the tip that would slice jaggedly into flesh and necks, ensuring her goal when chopping off a head, a leg, or an arm.

The suit was like an apparel version of an armored car and had been cut to fit her body perfectly. She snapped her black and silver blade into place across her back and secured her SAF .45 and silencer, with three extra clips of ammunition. The weapon was fairly new, TOP's newest addition to their growing gun collection. Wig on head and weapons in place, she was ready to take on whatever monster made the mistake of underestimating her.

The handheld grappling hook device, an extension of her suit, resembled one of Batman's toys. A harder, more durable material wrapped around her shoulder and upper back like a snug-fitting sleeve and provided lifting support. The only exposed part of the device was being controlled by her hand.

According to the additional information she had burned out of Drago, she needed to get up to the eleventh floor of the Harrington Building. While Neal was on a sleep break during their sex marathon, she'd sneaked away to have a brief meeting with Drago.

Sevyn aimed the instrument with a five-story reach. Once the finger-sized hook was embedded into the concrete side of the building, she tugged the tiny metal cable that would be holding her weight. She tested its strength, astounded that something so thin was so strong. The tensile strength of the metal must have been off the charts.

Squeezing the small metal portion of the device attached to the palm of her hand, allowed her to activate, aim and shoot the cable, and retract it. She became airborne in an instant and loosening her grip reduced the speed at which she zipped up the wall.

The same night she had received the suit three months ago, she had snuck out and scaled several high rises. Once she reached the fifth floor, she aimed and anchored herself to scale five more stories. Before redeploying the device, she observed the outer perimeter of the building, noticing that the eleventh floor was the only one that showed movement. The sight reconfirmed her decision to enter the building on level ten.

Drago hadn't furnished her with any additional information about this building, but she didn't plan to leave until she found something substantial. If there were no monsters here, she would at least snoop around until she found information on the one monster she wanted most —Linkin.

The closer she rose to the tenth floor, the more frenzied her urge to kill grew, confirming that there were monsters here. She was clueless as to what triggered her urge to kill, but the need was flaring up like an internal fire that would only be extinguished with blood.

After unhooking her device, she retracted it, catching the small hook in her palm before hearing it lock into place. If forced to make a fast getaway, the bad guys wouldn't expect her fast pace, or her ability to jump from a tenth-floor balcony.

On this particular balcony, she noticed the lion statues. They sat with their chests puffed up and heads regally set like they were standing guard. A roving glance revealed that only the balcony she stood on possessed the protective statues. Did they represent something?

The night was alive with a chilling silence. The wind swept past her ears, whispering softly like it was warning her to avoid something she couldn't see. The only movement was the fat rolling clouds occasionally revealing the full moon peeking at her like a giant eye in the sky.

Of course, the balcony door would be locked, but thanks to TOP's research and development team, she had equipment that would help her gain entry. The small cutting device no bigger than a cigarette lighter would cut through the glass like a hot knife through butter.

She cut a small square in the bottom of the glass wall next to the sliding glass door. The opening resembled a doggy door, cut behind a set of thick curtains that would help conceal her entry, and make for a fast, somewhat hidden getaway, if she had to run.

Sevyn sat the glass square away from her passageway and slipped into the room. She found herself inside an apartment, which could explain the statues on the balcony. Stone statues similar to the ones on the balcony sat in place inside the apartment as well.

In the dim lighting, she easily recognized leather sofas and chairs, crystal vases, and handcrafted art pieces. Italian-styled furnishings lined the place with linear precision. She snooped but didn't find anything worthwhile before exiting the apartment.

The sharp contrast between the dimness of the apartment's interior and the light in the hallway made her more aware of her surroundings. Thankfully, the hall was clear, so she made her way to the stairway that sat on the end like a doorway leading to another dimension.

Tiptoeing up the stairs, the closer she drew to the next level, the more it gave her clues as to what was happening. The muffled sound of music and laughter greeted her before she opened the door. She prepared to navigate another long hallway and her speed allowed her to breeze through the passage with ease.

Within seconds, she reached the double doors that led into the party taking place, but like everything around this place, the doors were locked. She smiled. Her new suit came with a tiny blowtorch, and it took seconds to melt away the lock.

She inched the door open and found people everywhere; so many, their scents camouflaged the monsters. The only reason she knew monsters were among the humans was because her blood boiled to kill them.

Unfortunately, the only way she knew to distinguish them among the crowd was to get up close and personal. She didn't want to make her presence known, nor could she cause a scene that could accidently kill an innocent person who, in this moment, didn't know they were a part of the menu.

Sevyn turned away from the door, preparing to ease it back closed, but the sudden quiet called to her as loud as the noise seconds ago. The music and the crush of the crowd had come to an abrupt stop. She turned back, her movements slow and cautious. Had the monsters spotted her? Smelled her?

The scene inside the room wasn't something she'd ever seen before. The people all stood eerily still, staring at a projected image on the wall before them. Whatever the pale face on the screen was saying, Sevyn couldn't hear it, but the people were tuned into every word.

The monsters had them under some type of sway, similar to what she had done to Neal. However, there were three in the crowd glancing around at their frozen friends, confused.

Where were the monsters? Why weren't they showing themselves? The two men and the woman who weren't under the trance were starting to panic, stumbling around the room, attempting to shake their friends awake.

"What's going on?" one of the guys asked.

"What the hell is wrong with everyone? Is this some kind of joke?" the woman questioned, her shaking voice carrying through the room.

"This way," a deep male voice called to the three who remained lucid. "If you can hear my voice, come up on the stage, please."

Was this how the monsters decided who they would eat? They wanted the ones who weren't susceptible to hypnosis. They wanted their food alive and kicking.

She couldn't let those monsters eat those people.

Her roaming gaze landed on the fire alarm. A devious smile bent her lips as she sent her grappling hook into the nearest light fixture, smashing it. She retracted her device and smashed another light, for good measure, making the immediate area outside the exit darker.

She sneaked around and barred the front door, ensuring she would herd the partygoers in her direction. The back hall she was using didn't have an elevator, so she propped open the door to the stairwell.

Her aim was to take accurate inventory of the monsters as they exited. She pulled the fire alarm, hoping the loud, wailing sound disrupted the trance the people were stuck in and sent them running out the door.

She'd used her device to boost and post herself above the doorway and clung to the surface like a waiting spider. When the sound of movement started to blend with the fire alarms shrieking yells, a satisfied smile filled her face.

The stampede of people started to pour from the room, the rapid beats of heels and shoes making the area around her vibrate. Her face creased in tight irritation when none of the monsters exited among the remaining people rushing out the door. Were the monsters on to her ploy?

Once the alarm stopped and the last two people scurried down the stairwell, one of the monsters appeared and stood directly below her position. His head moved in every direction, searching, like he sensed her.

"We know you're here. I caught a whiff of your scent the moment this door opened. Clever, getting rid of the humans." The searching monster spoke into the hallway. "We've all been put on alert that there was a hunter in this city, so we expected to run into you sooner or later."

Now that a monster stood below her, Sevyn's odd angle had her grip tightening around the slipping rope of the grappling hook. The darkened hallway assisted in keeping her hidden, but why hadn't she done more weight training like she'd planned to and dropped that extra ten pounds?

The man stood in place, staring around for a lingering moment, unintentionally dragging out her agony. When he decided to move, he propped the doors open and thankfully stepped back into the room.

Sevyn took his gesture as an invitation and jumped from her position, using her speed to surprise the man who had taken a few steps into the room. He turned with his hands up but was too late. She sent Queen slicing through his neck so fast, he was unable to utter a sound in protest or warning.

His head hung unnaturally off his shoulders at a forty-five-degree angle, leaving a wide, gaping hole of blood and exposed flesh. The monster was in such distress, his face, even while his neck hung nearly off his shoulders, expressed his gripping fear.

Sevyn was poised to send her blade the rest of the way through his neck but was gripped harshly from behind. She didn't struggle against the firm hold. Instead, she leaned forward and snapped her head back with such force, she prayed she had broken multiple bones in its face.

The hit was a good solid one that resulted in her quick release.

She was now surrounded by four monsters whose spicy ginger scent swam up her nose and invaded her lungs with the toxic potency of poison.

CHAPTER TWENTY

SEVYN

THE FOUR CREATURES used military precision to close in on her while she turned in a circle, aiming her blade at them. They drew closer, inch by careful inch, their gazes locked on her, their fists clenched and their bodies racked with tension.

Her hands shook, but it wasn't from fear. The struggle to stave off her impulsive urge to kill was an immeasurable ache that stabbed down to the bone. The need had the strength of an unnamed drug that ravaged her mentally and physically.

She continued to spin at a leisurely pace, taking in their positions and attempting to read their intentions. Was it nervousness and fear she saw projected in their facial expressions and taut body postures? Were they afraid of her?

Drago had been right. There were monsters here. Unfortunately, none of them was Linkin. At least she would get a chance to ease her urge and rid the world of some of these blood-drinking leeches.

With Queen poised masterfully in one hand, Sevyn used her speed to draw and aim her gun. Her aim was off due to the grappling device attached to her palm, so she adjusted.

She loved seeing the surprise she left on the monster's faces when they first grasped that she was as fast as, and sometimes faster than they were. The one with the low cut beard and tall, skinny body, had gone stock still while the others, more bulky and equally as tall, took up defensive postures.

"We don't want any trouble. We've heard about you and we have nothing against you and your kind. We're trying to live in peace."

My kind?

Sevyn blew out a loud huff. "Trying to live in peace by inviting a bunch of humans to your parties without divulging that they're the buffet? You're cannibals and monsters, the worse kind of killer, and you deserve whatever you're going to get."

The negotiator continued to talk, but Sevyn stopped listening.

She ran, blade-first, into the one in front of her, sending the cold, hard metal through his chest. Her rapid movement sent the other two back a few paces.

As quickly as her blade plunged into her target's body, she was turned by a strong force and spun savagely by one behind her. His rough handling helped with the retraction of her blade, unintentionally giving her more pulling force.

When her blade forcefully jerked from its body, out flew chunks of what she discerned were his heart. Sevyn didn't wait around to see how badly she had damaged it. She slung her bloody blade blindly, striking the monster that held her from behind.

As soon as Queen was planted into a body part, she fired at one of the two in front of her, hitting one in the head. The head shot dropped him, but his jerking body revealed that he wouldn't be down for long.

The blade was planted deep in the one hanging onto her from behind with a death-grip around her neck. Unable to jerk her blade free, she was forced to strain her arm at an unnatural angle in order to hang on to the handle. She refused to let go, even as his forearm cut off her air supply, and the pull on her blade threatened to snap her arm.

Another ran towards her with his gaze aimed at her legs, giving away his plan. The impact from the bullets she released slammed into his forehead, snapping his head back with maximum force. The chest shots she gifted him with jerked his body back a few feet, the powerful punch of the bullet's impact sounded off like drumbeats.

She may have been in a chokehold, but not all of her functions had been subdued. She maintained her tight grip on her stuck blade and dropped, letting her body fall to the floor.

Using her weight did the trick in setting her blade free, but the force also sent her to the floor hard enough, the impact knocked her breath away. Breath or no breath, the fall didn't stop her from shooting at what was in front of her. The one she shot earlier hobbled closer, holding his chest. The hole in his forehead was visible but not bleeding. The one who'd held onto her was behind her now, moaning and groaning.

She spun on her butt, swung, and sent Queen through his calf. The vibration of the blade's impact let her know she had struck bone. The scream the thing released made the hair on her neck stand.

Since the thick blade was planted deeply, she yanked hard enough to send the man tumbling to the floor. Queen refused to give up the bone it had bit into and remained sticking out of the man's leg. By the time his body joined hers on the floor, two slugs from her gun introduced themselves to his head and two more pierced his chest.

Sevyn dropped her empty clip and reloaded with lightning speed, but her gun was knocked from her hand before she could incapacitate the last two. One roughed her up from the back, shoving his forearms under her arms while the other clutched her ankles. Her blade remained embedded in the leg of the one writhing in pain on the floor, making her regret not bringing her extra blade, King along to protect her and taste some of this blood.

They were taking her, dragging her off somewhere without weapons. If she didn't take their heads soon, they would heal, and she couldn't allow that to happen. She struggled to break free, but the monsters had the advantage. Sevyn may have been faster than some, but they were much stronger.

They were speaking again, but she had a one-track mind when it came to these things. Her eyes landed on her gun, which had been flung across the room, and on her blade, planted in the leg of the downed monster.

Bucking ferociously, Sevyn, struggled to break free of the two holding her. The downed freaks were starting to recover already, and her work was going to waste.

One of the two carrying her yelled to get her attention. "We're not your enemy. Did you notice we were not trying to kill you until you went after us?"

"Everything in my blood tells me we are very much enemies," she spit at him while continuing to try to jerk herself free. "You don't want to kill me because you want your food alive when you eat it. And let's not forget the people you were planning on eating and drinking. If you're stupid enough to not fight for your soulless lives, that's your business. I want to rip your hearts out and chop your heads off, so I can look into your tortured eyes as you burn into ash."

"Man, she is as brutal as they say," one had the nerve to say.

His statement put a wrinkle in her forehead. Did they all know about her?

Her struggling ceased, and Sevyn stifled a smirk. A plan had emerged. She also noticed that neither of them responded to her comment about them slaughtering and eating people without remorse.

One monster supported her under the arms which, thankfully, left her hands dangling. She twisted her wrist until she found the angle she wanted. If she could line up her hand just right, she might be able to free herself. She let loose a low groan as they approached the propped open doors. A frown creased the face of the one with her feet in his tight grip.

His stare grew more intense, and his frown deepened. "What are you—"

The rest of his question never sailed past his lips.

Sevyn sent the grappling hook into the wall nearest her gun. She squeezed the retracting device, and her body lurched from their grips. She went flying through the air the first few feet before sliding on her butt the rest of the way across the floor, zooming by the first one she had dropped. As she skidded by the second one, she gripped and snatched her blade from his leg.

She eased her grip on the retracting lever, slowing in time to stop herself from slamming into the wall, but the force of her pull wasn't working in retracting the device from the wall. It was stuck. She didn't have time to unhook the device the old-fashioned way, but thankfully, she had enough play in the wire to reach her gun and take aim at the two coming her way.

One dove behind a large table. The other was too far in the open to hide as one of her slugs missed his head. A second shot landed in his chest, knocking the top portion of his body back. The bullet slowed him, but he continued his approach, and she sent him sliding to the floor with two more shots into his chest.

Finally, she jerked and snatched hard enough that the grappling hook was pulled free of the wall, allowing her to retract it, aim, and shoot it versus the gun. The hook shot into the right eye of the wounded and approaching monster. It pleased her to see him scratch at his wounded eye, his face scrunched and showing open-mouthed disbelief at what she had done.

Since the hook was embedded in his head, she retracted the device and his body came sliding, headfirst, towards her. She sat with Queen raised high, waiting for his head to get within striking distance.

He stopped before his head hit her right angle. Kicking him repeatedly, she forced his body into position before sending the blade into his neck. His suffering screams vibrated her eardrums, the sound a musical melody as she hacked through his neck with pride and without prejudice.

She glanced up in time to see the one who had ducked out of the way of her merciless attack running from the room. She didn't waste time chasing after him as the rest of his friends had nearly recovered. It was probably a good idea to let one get away. Hopefully, he was scared enough to exaggerate what he had witnessed tonight, and by the time her story reached his friends, she would be the big, badass monster they should all be afraid to meet.

Sevyn had to collect the heads now or be forced to start the incapacitation process again. She used speed and their weakened states to hack away two and a half more heads. She'd never taken four heads at once, so she took a moment to situate them before preparing to leave the building.

She considered leaving the easy way by going through the lobby but didn't have a good enough story to explain to lobby security why she carried four decapitated heads.

Speaking of lobby security, why hadn't they shown up?

She shrugged and got back to work, figuring they likely worked for the monsters and had been ordered not to disturb their buffet party.

The small sack she'd pulled from her upper sleeve pocket and carried specifically for head collection was stuffed with three of the four heads. The last head wasn't so lucky. His hair was too short for her to grip, so she sank her fingers into the mush of its butchered neck to get a grip. The moans and screams the head released were toe-curling and unholy, vibrated off her skin, and made her want to scratch the exposed areas.

There wasn't time to muzzle the condemned beings as she returned to the tenth floor. The heads were a choir of pleading cries and yells. They were all begging to be spared, promising they weren't dangerous creatures.

Sevyn made it back to the apartment without a problem and shoved the sack of heads through the small cutout. She and the head dangling from her fingers like a bowling ball couldn't slide through the opening at the same time. Unsnapping her blade, she spiked the head, and tossed it through the opening before she shimmied through.

Once on the balcony, Sevyn silently assessed her surroundings. The strange sense of being watched washed over her. Unpiking the head from her blade, she stood, poised to fight whatever decided it wanted a piece of her.

The only sound came from the faint drip-drop of blood falling from her blade. Even the heads were quiet, which she found peculiar. After waiting for what felt like an eternity, she strapped Queen in place, gathered her heads, and prepared to grapple her way back down the building.

Finding the ground level clear, she hiked back to her car a half-mile away and headed to the warehouse. Her impending task left her insides buzzing with anticipation, the images of the faces of death already forming in her head. She had some burning to do, and she planned to enjoy every second.

At five in the morning, she had an hour to clean up and take a quick nap. The idea of climbing into bed with Neal was a pleasant one.

After a long, hot shower, she slinked into the bed. Neal

greeted her with open arms when she lowered her head onto his chest and let her heavy body melt into his welcoming warmth.

"How many did you kill?"

His question was unexpected. Surprising. However, if there was anything she was learning about Neal, it was that he wasn't one of those guys that treated her like she wasn't capable of handling herself. The memory of how he'd stood by on the bridge and allowed her to handle her business sat at a reserved table in her mind. He'd only assisted when she'd asked or when he believed her life was in jeopardy.

"How do you know I was out hunting?" she replied, with a question of her own.

He sat up. "Drago gave you a lead last night that you never mentioned again. You snuck out of here when you thought I was asleep. My guess, to torture more Intel out of Drago.

"When I woke up and noticed you were gone, I figured you went to check it out. I'm worried about you, Dana, even though I know you can handle yourself. I also know that nothing I say, or do, will stop you from hunting the monsters that murdered your mother. I just want you to know that I'm here for you, no matter what, no matter how dangerous."

She liked that he exhibited genuine concern for her. What she liked better was that he didn't try to make decisions for her or tell her what to do. It was a quality that made her respect him that much more.

"I appreciate that more than you know." A smile found its way onto her face, her lips turning up into a pleased grin. "I took four heads tonight. You should have heard the dreadful commotion they made while I forced them to watch me burn their friends' heads."

Neal pinned her with a lingering stare that stalled her words. "I say this with no negative connotation intended, but after meeting Sevyn, I am not sure if Dana is who you truly are. You're beautifully frightening and should be called Dana-Sevyn.

You have the essence of a princess in Dana, but your soul has been touched by death in Sevyn."

She smiled, unbothered by the comment. "Thank you."

Neal laughed. "The fact that you took that as a compliment validates my statements."

Dana's gaze shot up to the ceiling. She imagined she could be a bit disturbing and scary at times, but she strived to make up for it when she wasn't hunting monsters.

Worry crept into the corners of Neal's eyes as he checked out her bruises, running a gentle hand over them. "Are you in pain? Those look like they hurt."

They were the kind of war wounds she didn't mind one bit and wore with pride.

"For four of their heads, every bruise is worth it."

Neal drew her onto his chest and kissed the top of her head. The gesture was so sweet and sincere, it relaxed her body and mind. She was sure that killing monsters took pieces of her soul, but she was starting to believe Neal was the key to restoring the missing parts.

He had no idea he provided her with the most peaceful place in the world. She needed to watch her step with Neal. He was making it too easy for her to fall for him.

CHAPTER TWENTY-ONE

DANA

TEN DAYS HAD ZIPPED by since she and Neal had revealed their secrets to each other. Now, they were joined at the hip, and not only because he was her protection. Dana wanted him around. Day by day, she was developing a need for him. Having discovered that they had so much in common like their abilities and the organization they worked for, drew them to each other like magnets. He was the first man in her life that she could be herself with, and he'd admitted relishing the same freedom with her.

There was a bond strengthening between them that left her questioning what they were to each other. Great sex was one thing, but Dana felt something between them that kept gripping her tighter and dragging her in deeper. Were they a couple? There were times when it certainly felt that way although neither of them would speak on the matter.

They were practically sharing her room, and the times he remained in his room at night, she'd creep next door and climb into bed with him. Although she sensed his memories were a touchy subject for him, he allowed her to conduct several mental exercises with him in an attempt to coax them back.

Now, in the middle of bumper-to-bumper traffic, Neal maneuvered around vehicles until they came to a stop. An accident up ahead stopped their trek to work, so Neal shifted the car into park. Dana didn't mind it. Time alone with him was fine with her.

"I don't think we're going anywhere, anytime soon," he stated, stretching his neck to get a good look ahead of them.

Dana repositioned, turning in the seat so that she faced Neal. She put her legs up on the seat with her back resting against the door panel. After kicking off her heels, she laid her head against the glass and placed her feet against Neal's muscled thigh. He could see straight up her skirt and judging by the way his eyes skimmed up her legs, he enjoyed the view.

He wrapped a strong hand around her right foot. The pleasing pressure of his thumbs massaging the arch caused her to relax further into the door panel. Not even the door's armrest poking her in the back bothered her while Neal was massaging her foot. He knew how to make all her worries disappear with a touch.

"That feels good. You have magical hands," she complimented, wanting him to keep going.

His strong hand glided up her leg. His smile was a reply to the soft moan she released. "You're ruining me, you know. I'm not going to be any good for any other woman," he said. The honesty in his statement shined through his eyes. Neal was of a different breed. He said what he meant, and she liked it.

"Good," she replied. "It means I get to keep my claws in you."

He paused, his penetrating gaze holding hers. "Are you sure you want to go into the office? You've hardly had any sleep in the last week with the amount of hunting and stakeouts you've been doing."

There were some missions Neal had accompanied Sevyn on and some she'd sneak away in the middle of the night to carry out alone.

"I'll be fine. I've gotten used to getting by on little sleep." She sat up and glanced around, noticing traffic hadn't moved an inch. "I'm sorry for getting you stuck in this mess of traffic. But when given the option of being on time or sex with you, I couldn't resist choice number two. We could have left an hour ago if it weren't for my overactive libido."

A smile lit up his face before his tongue glided across his sexy lips. "Dana. Dana. Dana. You have no idea how good this feels. To have a woman like you acknowledge me with interest, it's almost too good to be true."

She liked him. He had a quiet way of siphoning emotions from her, some she didn't know she possessed. And he said the most unexpectedly sweet things. Dana rose and kneeled next to him, placing the front of her body at his side. She couldn't help running her hand along his wide and strong shoulders until her fingertips brushed the hair at the back of his neck. Her fingers glided over the goosebumps her touch left on his skin, the revelation sparking a strong impulse of unexpected emotions.

She ran her hand along his nape until her fingers raked through his baby soft hair. His eyes fell closed against the soft caress of her fingers. He was unaware that the mere sight of him drew her in, so much so, she feared the way her emotions surfaced to lavish him with affections she did her best to hide.

She sat higher on her knees, pressing her body deeper into his side, wanting to kiss him so badly she bit her bottom lip and kept it trapped between her teeth. He wanted to kiss her too, she could tell, but there was also worry hidden within the depths of his eyes.

"I don't think we should be this close in public," he suggested.

The impact of his words was crushed under the weight of their closeness. Her right leg slipped across his lap, forcing her skirt up and her backside to brush the steering wheel. The warmth of his strong hand rested against her waist after it automatically lowered to that area.

"What's wrong? What's bothering you?"

His gaze seared into hers, melting her senses and locking her in place. The strength of his emotions seeped from the depths of his gaze. Closed within the confines of his strong caress while being pressed so securely against him was like nothing she had ever experienced. Their connection gave off an untamed energy that made her stomach come alive with butterflies last night and every time since their first time together. However, this time, her stomach clenched with so much anxious energy, it made her jittery.

Stunned by the force of the galvanizing power, they remained locked in the reciprocated trance they had on each other. His gaze remained fixed on hers, the penetrating glint in his beautiful eyes reaching down to her bones. That's when she spotted *it*, a mix of every emotion named, powered up and aimed at her. This was the first time he'd let her see him like this, open and extremely vulnerable.

The strong pull he possessed over her senses kept her face hovering slightly above his. She wasn't the only one with the ability to sway others because Neal had her under his spell. If she kissed him, truly kissed him, with this much emotion driving her, there would be no turning back. If she were being truthful with herself, the damage had already been done the first time she'd let him touch her.

Her mind dragged in his last statement about him and her being close in public.

"Are you telling me to stop? I don't take rejection well."

He didn't answer but tracked her movements as she lowered her lips to his. The delicate press of the soothing caress of his soft lips gave her mouth a new purpose. She stole his breath one second and lost hers the next, but it didn't stop her desperate need to live within the sensual flow of their immeasurable kiss.

Neal's words edged through the choir of their harsh breaths. "Why me, Dana?"

Her brows pinched tight.

"What?"

"Why me? You're beautiful. Wealthy. Strong. You can have anyone you want. Are you having fun with me?"

Her brows knitted deeper. Did he not feel their chemistry? Did he not notice that she had been clinging to him like they were a legit couple for the past couple of weeks? Had he not felt the shift between them even as far back as the elevator encounter? And if she was being honest with herself, he'd sparked her intrigue from the moment she'd shook his hand.

"Why are you asking me this? Do you regret us being together?"

He shook his head. "No. But, why me?"

She considered the question, squinting her eyes at him. "Why not you? Are you saying that you're not deserving of a beautiful, strong, and wealthy woman?"

His hands tightened around her waist.

"Do I need to spell it out? I'm damaged. Most women see my face and stare like I'm one of the monsters you hunt. You pretend there's nothing wrong with me. I can tell that you're attracted to me, but I don't understand it. I believe its genuine, so it confuses me."

Dana took a deep breath, unsure how to explain her side of their situation. Her aching hand rested against his neck while she used her thumb to tilt his head up so that their faces were aligned. A light tremble started in her hand the moment their gazes connected. The labored breaths that escaped told on her and gave him a glimpse of how she overflowed with emotions for him.

His eyes searched hers while she scanned his, telling him with a look what she was too afraid to put into words. Had this uncontrolled *thing* hidden between them been there the entire time?

They jumped.

A horn blowing behind them sounded, but their eyes never strayed from each other despite the disturbance.

"Neal, I don't see you as damaged. When I look at you, I see a strong, vibrant, confident man who is also considerate, affectionate, and mindful of my feelings. I don't pretend that nothing is wrong with you. In my eyes, there's nothing wrong with you."

Dana reached to caress his scar, but Neal turned his face away from her hand. She turned it back.

"Let me ask you this. The way women look at your face, or stare at your scar, has it ever stopped you from getting a woman into bed?"

He bit into a wide smile. "No, not really."

"Are you sure you haven't been misreading what you think women see in you?"

He shrugged. "I've never cared before."

Now, she understood.

"I haven't mentioned your scar because I see past it. I see you, Neal. Only you."

Her palm rested against his scar, the reassuring touch adding validity to her words. She traced the puckered and discolored flesh, every inch of it. Her searching gaze stared into the depth of his, the intensity of the potent action allowing their emotional exchange to reach out and touch. The connection created a force so palpable she swallowed hard and whimpered from the explosive effect it had on her heart.

"You never have to care about how any other woman looks at you. They will never see what I see. They will never know what I know. They will never want you the way that I want you."

She kissed him, leisurely and lovingly. She wasn't sure she was ready to tell him the part about her being in love with him, but there was that also. She didn't notice when it happened, but she was helpless against its power and the fact that there wasn't shit she could do about it.

The blaring chorus of horns lured her lips away from his.

"Do you understand me now?" she asked him in a breathless whisper.

She traced his scar, one last time, before placing her lips against it. Neal collapsed into her arms, and she folded them tightly around him, embracing him along with the strong emotions he stirred within her. The same ones she saw reflected back at her from the depths of his heavy gaze.

Bam...Bam...Bam.

The pounding vibrated against the side of her car, making them jump up and break away from their tight embrace.

With an irritated glare, the driver of one of the cars behind them stood staring.

Neal rolled down the window to the angry faced man already in the midst of his venting session.

"If you don't mind breaking up your little love affair, the rest of us would like to get to work. Four blocks up the road, there's a good hotel. Maybe you two should check in and get the hell off the streets."

The man was ticked off, so Dana suppressed her urge to laugh.

"Sorry, sir. We're moving."

She unglued herself from Neal, so they could stop blocking traffic. The man marched back to his car and wheeled it with sharp, jerking turns. He sped past them, taking his anger out on his engine.

Dana appreciated the interruption because she'd been a few breaths short of telling Neal about the one emotion she felt towards him that she was most afraid to admit. It was too soon. Too fast. Was she overthinking their relationship? Was she reverting back to her old relationship ways and forcing it to be something it wasn't? *We're just having a good time,* she told herself.

She stilled in the passenger seat when an overwhelming sense of calm flowed over her, luring her mind and body into quiet harmony. It was the kind of contented peace she'd only experienced from her association with Neal Erickson.

CHAPTER TWENTY-TWO

NEAL

UPON ARRIVING at Dana's office building, Neal sensed the dozen cop cars out front had something to do with Sevyn and her secret head-taking missions. He noticed her hesitant steps as they entered the elevator.

"I have a bad feeling my night job has finally spilled into my day job. I'm praying those cop cars have nothing to do with me."

They exited the elevator and were stopped in their tracks by the booming voices of the two officers posted up at the end of the hall leading to her suite. One kept a tight grip on his baton and glared at Neal while Dana explained her position to his partner. They weren't granted a pass until after the partner studied Dana's identification as heavily as he'd eyed her up and down.

Neal glanced back, giving the officers a *fuck you* glare while stalking down the hall towards the suite. When they entered the lobby area, they froze. The place was in shambles, giving a hint to what the rest of her office would look like. Parts of the ceiling had been ripped out, and tiles and wires clung to what was left up there. Furniture had been flipped, and every object that had previously sat on a flat surface had been swept off.

Dana called her brothers, and while on three-way, their panicked voices projected loud enough for Neal to make out their side of the conversation on the phone. Although they worked in the same building their family owned, her brothers were upset that they were being denied access to Dana's floor.

Neal's boots thumped against the wet floor, creating a splash with each step. The sprinkler system had been triggered and then shut off, so the carpeted sections of the flooring mushed under his boots like a soaked sponge. The furniture was tossed about and desks, chairs, and paperwork was left in wet piles.

Jordan ran to Dana with tears spilling down her cheeks, her body visibly shaking. "I tried to stop them, but they were crazy. They tore up the place. I thought we were all going to die," she sobbed.

Dana attempted to relax Jordan with a reassuring voice and gentle hugs, but the woman was clearly in shock.

The other workers sat huddled near each other, wrapped in blankets and speaking in low murmurs. Any unfamiliar sound had them jumping and unconsciously ducking for cover. They were sequestered in the reception area and prohibited from leaving so they could be interviewed.

Dana released Jordan from a firm hug and rubbed her shoulders with delicate strokes.

"Please, slow down. Tell me what happened. Is anyone hurt?"

Jordan took deep and shaky breaths before she blew a long one past her trembling lips.

Dana attempted to gather information from Jordan while Neal observed the trashed area further to see if he could pick up clues as to who had done this.

When he walked into Dana's office, he stole a quick glance before one of the officers ordered him to join the rest of the group. The way Dana's office had been trashed Neal found it difficult to believe the monsters were responsible. From what little he knew of them they weren't this careless and reckless.

From the pace at which they were conducting their investigation, Neal doubted the investigators had already pulled the surveillance footage. As soon as the one nearest him turned his back, Neal disappeared, jumping back into Dana's office.

An hour later had gotten them a step closer to finding a few answers. If he and Dana didn't find the culprits, they would eventually find their way to her house. Thankfully, no one at the office was physically hurt. Based on Jordan's account, four gun-wielding men entered and overtook the front office clerk.

Once the employees were shoved into the conference room, they stood frightened, watching through the room's broken glass while the men tore up the place. Jordan was convinced the men were crazy because it sounded like they said they were looking for a dragon.

Upon hearing Jordan's shaky words, Neal and Dana agreed that the men were looking for Drago. Dana was right about one thing; her night job had finally spilled into her real life, and her entire family was in danger.

The more time Neal spent with Dana, the more respect he gained for her. She was a TOP agent, so she had a contingency plan for a contingency plan. She started the process of a series of arrangements she'd put in place to keep the monsters away from her family.

Impressed, he listened as she initiated the first plan that involved flying her family to safety away from Seattle. She phoned her contacts and used pictures of her torn apart office, complete with actors in place, leading her family to believe that they were targets for kidnapping and ransom. The ruse wasn't a complete lie.

In less than two hours, she had her family flying to safety. The actors she hired to pose as law officials pulled her brothers from their offices followed them home and waited while they packed. Her father was already abroad but still received word just as Dana had planned it.

She would receive reports, confirming when her brothers were safely in the air. She'd lied, informing her brothers and father that she was on her way to safety as well. Neal had conferred briefly with her father and, of course, he made Neal promise to take care of his daughter. William Diallo had no idea his little princess was calling the shots.

With her family safe, Neal didn't have to ask to know that nothing would stop Dana from unleashing her alter ego, Sevyn. Although he had no intention of stopping her, he was sorry for whoever, or whatever, got in her way.

Neal drove on the way back to Dana's house, stealing glances at her preparing for battle in the passenger seat. She adjusted her bun into a flat braid she pinned in place before pulling on a wig from her glove compartment. His neck swiveled back and forth, taking her in before returning his eyes to the road. Did she keep wigs readily available in case she needed to let Sevyn loose?

Although he never thought he would admit it, he liked Sevyn. After seeing the incident on the bridge, what was left of Dana's office, and her hunting expedition that had resulted in her stopping people from being slaughtered and taking four heads in one night, he believed Sevyn was a necessity.

Sevyn was raw, unapologetically brutal, and he sensed that getting between her and the hunt was likely a hazard to one's health. Dana confessed to acting, but Neal was confused about which persona she was pretending to be, Dana or Sevyn? The fact that he couldn't decide which he was more attracted to unveiled another layer to his personality.

"Is it okay if I call you Dana-Sevyn?" he questioned.

She laughed. "This isn't the first time you've mentioned Dana-Sevyn. Why would you want to call me that?"

"In getting to know you, I honestly don't know which one you truly are."

She leaned in and gifted him a quick peck on the cheek. "You're the only one who can call me that."

They returned to her house to change and pick up their gear. The guards were a part of the contingency plan and was notified that they were relieved, with pay, until further notice. The smooth manipulation of her family, the guards, and their house staff solidified for him that Dana was more in command of her actions than he'd initially suspected. Executing one of her plans could have, at any time, freed her from the performances she put on for her family's sake

Guns, knives, stealth gear, Sevyn's wigs, tech devices, and Drago's head were loaded into her car. Neal discovered that the Mercedes she usually drove was bulletproof. He was impressed by the arsenal of weapons she kept hidden in a secret trunk compartment and in a hidden floor panel behind the driver's seat.

While they'd changed, Dana informed Neal that she wanted to start the hunt at what she was assuming was Drago's house. They would also return to the Harrington Building, since they discovered it was a place the monster frequented. Sevyn had staked out the place every other night, searching for monsters until she'd caught one in the act of drinking a human. The individual, a forty-two-year-old father of two, was still in the hospital. It wasn't until Neal had witnessed the brutality the monsters lavished on humans that he better understood Sevyn's brutal nature towards them.

The place was crawling with monsters last night. She'd burned her newest victim to the point of him snitching and giving her what she hoped was Drago's address. There was no way he was babysitting Drago's head, so Neal drove. He found it difficult to understand how Sevyn endured Drago's repeated yelling and promises about providing leads to Linkin's whereabouts. His voice was nails pressing so hard on a chalkboard they were breaking, while his severed head sat on the seat next to Dana's hip.

The discerning sight of a functional body part without its body had all sorts of questions running through his brain. What type of magic was keeping him alive, aware, and animated while he was in two locations?

"I don't know where Linkin lives, but his number one guy lives at the Harrington Building. Did you check out the building?"

A sharp finger was aimed at his head. "Your little business venture turned up a group of your soulless friends. I found no trace of Linkin, and I couldn't make them cough up any substantial leads. As a matter of fact, none of them knew Linkin, but I did manage to burn an address out of the one I found there last night: 156 Falkner Boulevard."

The silence that filled the car left only the sound of the rubber kissing the road. Her smile surfaced and spread wide. Drago's silence confirmed she'd secured his actual address.

"You die today, Drago. I found you numerous times, and I'll eventually find Linkin. I hope you've made peace with whatever demon you worship." She lifted her phone to her ear. "Thirty minutes, Charlie. Torch the cold, headless one."

At that order, Drago screamed like a mad man, promising leads Sevyn no longer cared to hear.

CHAPTER TWENTY-THREE

SEVYN

SEVYN HAD HAD it up to her ears with Drago and his faulty leads. It was because of him that her employees could have been eaten or killed. He knew more than he revealed, but she didn't know how to get him to talk. He was willing to take his secrets to the grave, and she didn't mind helping him get there.

Now, they were heading towards his house to dig up clues that would lead them to Linkin. Neal's voice jolted her from thoughts of killing more monsters.

"We've picked up a tail, likely more of *his* friends. It appears they were staked out, waiting for us to make a move on his house."

A quick peek through the passenger's side mirror revealed two black Lincoln Town Cars. She prayed the big, beefed-up black Hummer speeding through traffic was late for a meeting and not a part of the convoy meant to follow them.

Neal's firm grip on the steering wheel was the last thing she caught before her body was flung forward and slammed back into her seat. Drago's head went rolling along the side of her leg while she fought to regain control of her body. The Hummer's engine roared, gearing up to ram them again.

Sevyn shoved the heel of her shoe into Drago's face, his skin and facial structure giving under the leg-shaking pressure she applied. The action helped hold her steady in her seat, and she relished the thrill of crushing his face under her shoe.

"You did this, you bastard. You knew we were rolling into a trap."

As they reached the peak of the Flotante Bridge, she didn't like the scene developing. The bridge was built unusually tall, crossing into the newly developed Flotante community. The area was a raised, manmade neighborhood of shopping plazas, businesses, and overpriced apartments and condos. From afar, the community appeared to float high above the water.

More bad guys approached from the opposite direction against the flow of traffic. In broad daylight, on a busy bridge, the probability of innocent people getting hurt was great. Her enemies were planning to use the bridge's limited escape routes to trap them.

She sank her heel into Drago's right eye, inflicting more pain.

He screamed at her, despite his pain. "You were going to kill me anyway, you bitch! Now, my brother is going to kill you, and I hope I'm around to see it. My earring is a tracker. I've been waiting for my brother to find me before your demonic ass burns what's left of my head."

Sevyn now understood why the convoy hadn't been able to track them down until now. They couldn't track them to her house. Not only were they purposely located in a dead zone, but she and anyone that worked for them were issued special comms devices that worked in the area. If anyone attempted to locate her by planting a tracker, it wasn't going to work. And if they had managed to narrow it down to her area, they couldn't get in without starting a war.

Drago's crew was left with the options of waiting for his tracker to come back online, staking out the last place they'd lost the ping of his signal, or posting up at the only bridge that led to his house. She drove her heel deeper into Drago's eye, causing his bloodcurdling screams to fill the cab of her car. Her and Neal's harsh breaths and the screeching tires joined the noisy chorus of their chaotic surroundings.

Neal maneuvered the car like a pro racer while she gripped the front bar and headrest and continued her attempt to send her heel through Drago's brain. It wasn't going to kill him, but it would cause him pain. This time, her anger was aimed at herself for letting the situation become so messy. Her family was uprooted and now Neal's life was in jeopardy because of her vendetta against these monsters.

The odometer climbed past eighty and the bad guys remained on their tail. Cars cleared a path like they had rehearsed their movements. A second blow hit her car and sent her body lurching forward. Just as quickly, the seatbelt snatched her back.

Neal fought the steering wheel, attempting to correct the car's deadly spin out, but it was no use. The Hummer hit them with enough force in the perfect spot to execute a pit maneuver. At their speed, they were headed for instant death. She may have had supernatural blood pumping through her veins but she was also human and could be hurt like one.

The side of the bridge grew closer, rushing towards them at a rate of speed that surpassed hers. Three things happened simultaneously, she closed her eyes, prayed, and clutched Neal's forearm, her nails digging into his flesh like that of a determined cat.

The crunch of metal and the bangs and snaps of her favorite car crashing into concrete invaded her ears. She and Neal were slung about as twisted metal punctured, stabbed, and pummeled them. Flying debris and glass aided in beating and battering them.

Although useless, she fought to shield her face behind the

bend of her arm. A sharp jerk sent Sevyn's head and elbow smashing into the side window. Her eyes flew open long enough to see that their momentum was substantial enough to keep the car moving to the only place it had left to go—over the side of the bridge.

Every bit of air she'd managed to drag in was sucked from her lungs when the car went airborne. The floating sensation hit like an aggressively thrown punch that forced her stomach into her chest. They were freefalling into the dark waters that waited below, waving and urging them to drop faster.

Sevyn's heartbeat pulsed in her throat. Her chest heaved for a single breath she couldn't seem to take. Drago's one good eye stretched wide with fright, searching frantically for an answer to why they had taken flight. Her hand squeezed Neal's, but he jerked his free from her desperate grasp. Snapshots showed him frantically freeing himself from his seatbelt.

What is he doing? We're about to die.

Once he was unbuckled, he climbed across the console and positioned himself over her. He straddled her legs before pulling her into a tight embrace in an effort to shield her from harm.

She admired his drive to protect her, but they were free-falling off the side of a bridge in a deadly drop. Covering her with his body wasn't going to save her. If the impact of such a fall didn't kill them instantly, the water, choppy and frigid, would finish them off.

Through all the turmoil, she sensed their energies connecting the moment Neal placed his mouth against her ear.

"I love you."

She never got the chance to reply due to her breath being snatched. Although she was experiencing the sensation of being torn apart, there was no pain, and her mind continued to produce logical thought.

She was dying and hadn't had the chance to tell Neal that she loved him back. She'd had many chances to tell him what she felt, but she'd let her stupid fear of a four-letter word deter her. Her brothers and father came to mind, along with fond memories of the time she'd spent with her mother. At least her family would be okay.

Sound, smell, sight, touch, and the bitter taste of blood in her mouth all surfaced at once, giving her the last snapshots of life. A floating sensation was quickly overpowered by a surge of energy she didn't have words to describe.

The next moment, she was rolling with no control of her body. Pain registered, a sharp reminder that she may have been alive as something hard dug into her flesh, scratching and scraping her with every turn.

Had she fallen free from the tumbling car? It should have been the death slap of the dark water cutting into her skin, not the hard, gravelly pricks poking at her now.

When she stopped rolling, her face landed against something warm and moving. She lifted her head, peeking through one eye and praying the accident had left her in one piece. The sight of Neal glancing down at her put an instant smile on her face.

Are we dead?

A quick glance at her surroundings suggested they were on the surface of the bridge. They heaved, fighting for every breath. The hard inhales and exhales burned her throat, but forcing precious oxygen into her lungs drew her full concentration.

Sevyn lay atop Neal, her mind in complete chaos. Images of the last few minutes flooded her memory banks. When she discovered her vocal cords were still functional, words flew from her mouth in a breathless rush.

"You did this. You pulled us from the falling car with your ability. You lovely genius. I lo—"

A red dot appeared on Neal's forehead. When she glanced

up, about ten well-armed men had them surrounded. The gear the men wore, and their precise tactical movements, implied they were well-trained and part of a paramilitary group like Drago had used on the bridge. If the monsters were using well-trained combat types, her mission to find her mother's killer would be that much more complex.

One asked, "Where is Drago?"

The sound of Drago's name floating through the air was enough to make her skin crawl. She couldn't contain her hate for that particular monster.

"He's dead. I had his body burned."

The man smirked at her admission. "No, we picked up his body in the nick of time. By the way, we didn't kill your mortician friend, Charlie. Despite what you may think, we're not all monsters."

It sounded like he was trying to convince himself more than her.

"Drago's head was in the car. The impact probably smashed it to oblivion."

The gun wielder laughed, the teasing sound heightening her irritation. Before she could get a word out, her worst horror was confirmed by a voice over the radio.

"We found his head. He's missing an eye, but he's going to survive once we return him to his body."

The man who did the talking flashed a condescending smile at Sevyn. "Darling, your friend, Drago will be all right. Tough bastard's got nine lives."

Sevyn growled, her teeth clenched to drive anger into the sound and the harsh gaze she shot at the man. He pointed a stiff finger at her, shaking it like he was preparing to discipline his child.

"You better be glad we saved him. If you had killed Linkin's last brother, there is no telling what he'd do to you. Pray we're not already too late because your actions may have triggered a war."

Sevyn had no idea what the man was talking about where it concerned starting wars, but she didn't take too kindly to threats, especially from humans who worked for monsters. She was as hot as a bed of disturbed fire ants because Drago was alive.

She sneered at the man. "You better be glad you're human and that I don't know your background. Otherwise, I'd find a way to kill you."

He didn't comment but curiosity seeped through the stern gaze he pinned on her. "How did you two get out of that car? I saw you inside before it went tumbling off the side of the bridge."

Sevyn cut her eyes at the man before allowing her head to fall against Neal's strong chest. Neal had been quiet the entire time, and if she knew him as well as she believed, he was trying to find a way out of this mess.

She was jerked up by two men, cuffed, and the muzzles of machine guns were shoved in her face by two more. What did these people think she was, a terrorist? A few brave bystanders ducked behind their cars but didn't miss out on the opportunity to film the situation with their phones. Their arms were extended like selfie sticks as they peeked around the bumpers and over the hoods of cars.

They handled Neal in the same rough manner in which they did her. Sevyn considered speeding away, but these guys had planned their setup well. There wasn't anywhere she could run that would lead her off the bridge, except for over the side, and she wasn't leaving without Neal.

She imagined she and Neal looked the part of the bad guys being apprehended by the authorities. The sheer number of armed military types compared to her and Neal in plain clothes was enough to keep people at bay. Her jerking resistance and the evil glares she flashed the men weren't going to garner any sympathy, either. People sat in their cars and gawked, unwilling to interfere in the situation as she and Neal were being carted away.

CHAPTER TWENTY-FOUR

NEAL

NEAL HAD no idea where they were being taken. He considered jumping, but wasn't going anywhere without Dana. They were chained like dogs in the back of an old white van. The van, with its dark tinted windows, reminded him of the type kidnappers favored back in the day.

Their captors were smart in not seating him within reach of Dana. His plan was to zap them out of the van, but he would need to have a physical hold on her first.

Back on the bridge, he'd had no idea if his plan would work when he couldn't stop the car from tumbling over the side of the bridge. He never thought it was possible to take another person into a jump with him, but he'd been desperate. The idea of Dana crashing to her death had been unfathomable, and he'd been willing to try anything to save her.

When the momentum of whatever propelled him through space sent him and her tumbling back to the top of the bridge, he realized he'd discovered a new twist to an ability he had once cast off as a hallucination. Being around Sevyn had him embracing and discovering himself, despite the many years he was missing.

Now, he was anchored to the metal paneling in the back of a hulled-out van. A black sack was thrown over his head, like the tinted windows weren't enough. Wherever they were being taken, it was a secret intended to be kept.

He wanted to jump next to Dana, so he could get them to safety, but his ability was stalled when they covered his head. If he couldn't see, nor had an accurate picture of where he would go, he was reluctant to act.

Although he didn't have it down to a science, he knew enough to know that he could leap into Dana's body, or a part of her body, and kill her. It was a risk he wasn't willing to take, so he sat in place, blind and filled with anxious energy.

Yelling and the van shaking indicated that Dana wasn't making the men's task of restraining her easy. The moment the struggling stopped; a small prick was the last thing Neal felt. They were being drugged, so he wasn't going to get the chance to guess where they were being taken after all.

DANA

Dana grunted, her vocal cries helping to stave off the stabbing ache in her head. Her frontal lobe had to have been under attack by brain-eating beetles. She sensed her and Neal's day from hell was far from over.

Holding her palm against her forehead, Dana raised her head and turned with caution to scan her surroundings. Where had they been taken? Thick bars hinted at a prison cell and her, the prisoner. The ache in her back told her she was lying atop a bunk with a mattress made of cement.

The walls were insane-asylum-white with a dingy cement ceiling. A dim light bulb hung from the ceiling, swaying on a tethered black cord. The dancing shadows cast from the light caused her dreary surroundings to rock against her vision. The mildew and stale air formed a bond to combat the scent of fresh blood. The faint sound of someone moaning drew her attention.

"Neal?"

He yelped and a moan followed, his pain dripping from his sluggish tone.

"Dana-Sevyn?"

He'd called her by the nickname he liked. Although she believed she was one person with a codename, he insisted that Dana and Sevyn were two different people. When she'd asked him who he liked best, he'd claimed he couldn't decide.

"Are you okay?" Her voiced rang weak but with concern.

"Yeah. Got a massive headache, but I'm okay. What about you?"

Dana cast a glance down her body, searching for injuries. "I'm great. It looks like I've landed us in a damn dungeon."

Her head continued to ache like it had been ripped apart and pieced together by a bunch of kindergarteners hyped up on chocolate. She forced herself to sit up fully, groaning with every move. The chamber she was confined in was copied straight from the dungeon of a medieval castle.

The front wall was fortified with thick and rusted iron bars and concrete. Dana forced her aching body to a standing position and limped towards the bars before peeking through the cracks. There was nothing but cement walls that created an eerily deserted hallway with two large iron doors at the end. Neal's low murmurs found her ears again.

"Neal, are you sure you're okay?"

"Yeah, I'm trying, but I can't use my ability. Otherwise, I would have gotten us out of here by now."

She attempted to use her speed, but nothing happened.

"I think they have us blocked. It's this place. I believe it has been ability-proofed, so we won't have a way to strike back at our captors. It means they know what we can do and likely have some gifts of their own."

"I used to think I was crazy. That my ability was a part of a psychotic break or hallucination. Now that I would like nothing more than to use it, we're stuck in a building that restricts it. Go figure."

Their low chuckles bounced off the solid walls despite their situation. Dana was thankful she and Neal hadn't been separated. Although she couldn't see him, knowing he was near relieved some of her stress. A slow, lazy smile bent her lips at the memory of Neal's admission when he'd believed they were free falling to their deaths.

"I love you."

DANA

Dana couldn't recall when she'd crawled back into the bed of rocks and fallen asleep until the *clink* of the lock and her whining cell door sounded and woke her. They were right about their abilities being muted. She couldn't use speed to get the upper hand on the approaching men.

She rose sluggishly, and not only did her head continue to pound, but her body also ached down to the bones. Whatever they had been injected with kept her drained of energy. Since she couldn't fight, she kicked uselessly, screamed, and acted a fool as the two men picked her up and carted her away. Two others dragged Neal from his cell, but unlike her, Neal remained calm.

"Put me down, you monster lovers. You're committing acts of terror against humankind by siding with flesh-eating, blood-drinking monsters. Put! Me! Down!"

She and Neal were carried through a dimly lit maze of halls

and sparsely furnished rooms. Although it was June and season-ably warm outside, the inside of this place could have doubled as a freezer.

Darkness covered the space, shielding it from being fully viewed and explored. Every once in a while, Dana noticed the flicker of a candle. Any visible item that gave off light was turned to the lowest possible setting. The small flames dancing atop the candles burned with a dim, lazy glow, barely skirting away the persistent darkness.

Neal's feet scraping against the stone floor sounded behind her. He remained the civilized one while she continued to yell and curse. She intended to resist all the way to—

"Where the hell are you taking us?" she shouted into the air.

They stopped abruptly, and the spicy ginger scent of monsters invaded her senses, triggering her insatiable need to kill. The human guards were turning her and Neal over to the monsters.

At first sight, these monsters were not like the ones she had encountered previously. These were unnaturally pale and garnered a certain level of sophistication in the way they walked and dressed. Their overall presentation was a statement in class. They sported tailored suits, shiny dress shoes, and were manscaped to perfection.

She never stopped assessing her surroundings while she continued her useless struggling. Her intention was to slow her captors down so she could see more and, hopefully, spot a way to escape this dark labyrinth.

They were in a mansion. A lair was a better word for it. From what she could tell, nearly everything was made of marble, granite, and a few other stones she couldn't identify by sight. She observed people milling about in the background, ignoring the commotion she was making.

Did the *men* of this place carry around women kicking and screaming all the time?

She lost her wig in her struggle, the Brazilian hair brushing over her shoulder on the way down to the floor.

Good.

She caught a glimpse of it before it was swallowed by the darkness. She never stopped struggling, even while taking pins from her hair. Having her hair down couldn't make her and Neal's situation any worse than it was, so she prayed it would at least distract these guards.

Neal flashed her a quick look, aware of what she was doing as she successfully wiggled away from one of the pale hands anchored under her right shoulder. Her partial freedom lasted seconds, but it was seconds she used to pluck free more of the hairpins and attempt to see where the hell they were being taken.

As they descended the stairs, darkness, thick and heavy, raked over her skin like the fingertips of a *rixie*. Dana's hair hung loose, the weight of it draped over her shoulders while tresses swung loosely through the air.

Was she being taken to the man in charge? The one she'd been chasing for years.

Each time Linkin crossed her mind, her blood began to boil, and her heartrate revved. Her anger gave her a spike of power that allowed her to snatch her foot free.

She took the opportunity to kick the guard in the face, sending her foot up with a speed that only her ability could have enhanced. Was it a shift in the atmosphere that caused her ability to reemerge or a shift within her? She didn't know but wasn't going to waste the opportunity.

She spun, jerking her arms free. The guards were stunned enough by her actions to pause, giving her the time she needed to formulate an escape plan.

With freedom as her motivator, she executed another rapid turn, grateful that her speed had given her the advantage. She kicked one of the men in the forehead and spun to gain enough momentum to thrust a vicious kick into the center of his chest. While the man was stumbling back from the first kick, she launched another into his stomach. His body kissed the floor with a loud thump.

Her next kick whipped through the air and crashed into the nearest glass table with lightning precision when the man rolled out of the way. The table shattered into thick, clattering shards.

Dana's actions caused a domino effect and Neal executed his escape, breaking away from the men who held him. He disappeared into thin air, causing the men to stumble around, dumbfounded. She caught a glimpse of him reappearing behind the fumbling men.

Not wasting a millisecond, she snatched up thick pieces of the broken glass in each hand from the table she'd broken. The commotion caused such a ruckus it drew in spectators, either visitors or residents of this place.

Neal delivered a hard shove to each of the men he'd disoriented with his disappearing act. Sevyn lifted and held the glass level with their chest, easily interpreting the set-up Neal created. The momentum from the push Neal delivered sent the men chest-first into the thick shards of glass she was proud to impale them with.

The wet crack their bodies made should have been disturbing, but Sevyn relished the sound, allowing it to feed her insatiable hunger to destroy them. Tiny splinters of glass bit at her palm and some dug in, but the six or seven inches that disappeared into her adversaries' chest cavity made her minor scrapes worthwhile.

Neal disappeared just as six more guards ran up, appearing to rush towards their location out of nowhere. Their chests heaved from the energy they must have exerted during their quick arrival.

Neal materialized behind Sevyn, his energy flowing over her skin like a delicate touch. They stood back-to-back, his strong back pressed against hers. Three guards faced Neal and three faced her.

He reached back and pressed his palms against her lower back. A deep breath seized her when he pushed her with a force she didn't know he was capable of unleashing. Before she crashed into the man in front of her Neal appeared behind him. He turned himself and the man out of her path so that she could take on another. Her elbow and fist worked at warp speed absorbing the hard flesh-breaking punches she delivered.

In her peripheral she caught a glimpse of Neal twisting the man's neck with enough force the loud crack found her ears and temporarily rendered the guard useless. He crashed to the floor in a heap, landing on his face before the rest of his body followed, limp and lifeless.

Sevyn's speed allowed her to land a well-timed fist to the jaw of the guard to her right. She followed the move up with a knee to the balls. It didn't matter that these guards weren't human, the rules where it concerned males, their dicks, and their balls, worked on most species.

The one she'd kneed folded over in pain, allowing her to send her elbow into the back of his neck. He hit the floor, his cheek screeching across the shiny marble. More spectators, at least ten were scattered around the area watching their fight at a distance, unwilling to get caught in the chaos she and Neal were delivering.

A shadow, one that read like a threat worse than the one's she currently faced, flashed across her peripheral. She spun, putting all the speed she possessed into the move. The blow was even further compounded when Neal appeared, grabbed a hold of the man, and helped his face meet her fist. The devastating blow nearly disconnected his mandible bone from his skull.

Neal and Sevyn fought in tandem like they were created to be the ultimate fighting partners. Her speed and his ability meshed like poetry. He created the verse, and she would complete the couplet.

Neal would spin, trip, and shove their adversaries, and Sevyn delivered vicious kicks, punches, and jabs that gave each piece of glass she found a purpose. One guard, who'd recovered from one of her blows to his face, attempted to stand.

Neal appeared behind the man. His mouth formed a wide O from the hard stomp Neal delivered to the backs of his legs, making him kneel before her. Sevyn swooped around the man like a vulture as soon as Neal blinked out of the way. She gripped and twisted the man's neck so hard; it gave off a wet *snap*.

Neal continued to line up targets, and she didn't hesitate to take them out. Within seconds they were down to the final three guards. Two of the three had cornered her, one at her back and the other in front of her with seething anger contorting his face.

Neal appeared before a big fist with bruised knuckles met her right eye. The momentum of the spin sent her tripping over a crumpled body, and she toppled to the floor. She rolled out of the reach of a foot coming at her head but didn't miss the opportunity to snatch up two pieces of glass within reach.

One of the shards was as long as her forearm and about an inch thick, the other was just as thick but shorter. Neal's surprising punches and kicks, most delivered at the moment he became visible, gave her a chance to stand and send the longest shard of glass harpooning into the jaw of one guard so forcefully, it scraped across his tongue and punched through to the other side of his face. His horror-infused scream whistled around the glass that pierced his face.

The next thing she knew, her hand had broken through his body. Determined, she shoved the shard so deep and hard into his chest, it punched clean through him and came out the back. The glass had made it through him, but her hand hadn't. Her actions caused the man to go unusually still, she supposed in an effort to combat the pain racing through him.

Her hand flexed while still inside him. She grasped that it was jammed against bone. Why hadn't she jerked her hand free of his body yet?

She had missed his heart in her hurried attempt to inflict damage but adjusted her hand, turning her palm down until she found her target. His heart was seated much lower than a human's. Her palm folded around his pulsing heart like a cage shutting in its prisoner. She didn't understand what drove her to reach for the organ. It was pure instinct. A sense of knowing she couldn't comprehend.

The monster continued to visibly hold his breath, his chest lifted high, his body tense and frozen. His unblinking, terrified eyes were locked on hers. The *thump* of his heartbeat as it pulsed inside her hand was the last thing she felt before she was gripped from behind, lost traction, and went flying into space.

CHAPTER TWENTY-FIVE

DANA

DANA WAS airborne and hurtling through the air at a rate that had her on a collision course with one of those stone walls. She was fast, but not fast enough to stop a midair toss by a monster strong enough to throw an SUV.

One of the monster's friends must have seen her with her hand inside the other's chest cavity, snatched her from behind, and tossed her like she didn't weigh an ounce.

She sensed the wall closing in on her head and braced herself for a major concussion or a possible skull fracture.

A *puff* sound whisked into her ear before her body was snatched in a different direction. Someone incredibly fast kept her from slamming into the wall headfirst.

The scent and the sensation of her savior was familiar. There was only one person who had the ability to make her feel warm and secure. There was only one person that could materialize virtually any place. She was in Neal's strong arms.

Swish.

They stopped so abruptly, her first order of business was to reacquaint her feet with the floor. A quick glance at Neal, standing before her, enticed her to smile, until she noticed the distressed look that creased his face. His eyes were laser-locked on her hand.

Dana hadn't noticed the movement inside her hand until she followed Neal's gaze. Her lips parted at the sight of a bleeding, quivering heart in her cupped palm, pulsing with life. Blood drizzled down her wrist as she fought to put order to all that had happened in the last few seconds.

The moment she'd understood she was palming the monster's heart; her intent *was* to jerk it from his chest, however, another monster had gripped and slung her in an attempt to save his buddy. The force with which she was jerked back and tossed must have helped her snatch the heart. When Neal saved her from crashing into the wall, the detached heart was transported with them.

She raised the heart level with her eyes, not believing all that had just occurred.

Pop!

Dana jumped at the unnatural sound. The heart had exploded with a soft pop, splattering her and Neal with blood. There wasn't time to analyze the details of the exploding heart because she was curious to see if the body belonging to the heart had exploded too? *Was this a new way of killing them?*

Glancing in the direction she'd been, a shadow crept across Dana's vision, making the hairs on her neck stand. A chill so cold climbed up her spine, it froze the bones of her vertebrae on the way up. Whatever lurked in the darkness was far more dangerous than any of the other monsters they encountered tonight. Neal stood at her side, his voice low and heavy from the thick tension that surrounded them.

"I don't know how it's being done, but they are blocking my ability to get us out of this tomb they call a house."

A vicious wave of dark energy dragged along her skin, lingering at the surface before it seeped in and caused her skin to tighten on her bones. The shadow peered from the darkest corner of the room, breezing across the distance in a blur with no distinguishable features. Neal's hand tightened around hers at the eerie sight.

It wasn't until the entity stopped moving that she caught a glimpse of its fingers, skeletal-like and so milky white they appeared to cut through the darkness and leave a blurry trail. He, or it, based on the slightest glimpse of its shadowed outline, was rail thin to match those boney fingers. *It* took another meticulous step in their direction. *Was it purposely keeping its features draped in darkness?*

Normally, Dana would have rushed forward or plowed into him, ready to do battle, but every instinct she possessed forced her to stay in place. Her and Neal's abilities were coming and going in unpredictable increments. The fission of energy that told her she was in control of hers had stopped tingling below the surface of her skin.

Neal's grip grew tighter around hers, sensing the deadly vibe emanating from what was lurking within the folds of darkness. Although the room was lit sparsely by flickers of fire from wall sconces and candles, the creature used whatever shadows were available to cloak itself. Its actions boggled her mind and made her question the state of her own reality.

Were the dim glimmers of light in the room playing tricks on her eyes?

It appeared the dark figure was drawing in the darkness and using it as a cloak. A corner of its pale face and right arm peeked from behind the black curtains it had formed, the darkness so intricately placed, she was sure she saw only what it wanted her to see.

Distracted by the figure, it took her a moment to notice everyone in the room, including the injured ones, had stopped moving. They all stared, as enraptured as her and Neal. Was this stalking figure the one who'd slung her across the room?

His entrance demanded their attention whether they wanted

to give it or not. When it allowed one half of its body to penetrate the darkness, Dana took a step, but Neal pulled against their tight grip to keep her in place. He must have assumed she was about to start a fight, but she only sought to get a better look.

The closer it got, the more the monster's presence called to her in a way she didn't understand, tugging on some untapped connection she didn't know was there. She was drawn to this dark figure, even as she fought a demanding urge to send it to hell.

The figure continued to control the darkness, manipulating it in some strange way by controlling the amount of light surrounding him. He was undoubtedly the most shocking, and perhaps most dangerous thing in the room, so why wouldn't he reveal himself completely?

The warm press of Neal's hand wrapped around hers kept Dana grounded. The creep factor in this scene was on overload. She glanced around, waiting for someone to drop dead or for something to burst into flames. She sensed it like she did the creatures she hunted; some great traumatizing event was about to happen.

A loose strain of her hair sailed away on a gust of strong wind before fluttering against her cheek. It was him. The figure was incredibly fast and stood in front of her before she gathered, he'd even moved.

She couldn't decide which happened first, her going airborne or her losing her breath. Both happened so quickly, she didn't have time to react to the fact that she'd been snatched. The firm grip Neal had on her hand had been useless.

The dark one had taken her, and there wasn't a thing she could do about it. Dana sat across his thin, but strong arms, and her own arms had somehow found their way around his neck, holding on for dear life.

She was fast, but this monster was twice as fast. Normally, when she used her speed, she saw actual shapes as she zoomed by objects. Now, all she saw were flashes of light and darkness. When the bottom dropped from her stomach, she knew they were airborne.

Was he some kind of bat or winged creature that had the ability to fly?

A sharp turn caused her neck to whip, and her cheek struck his collarbone, but just as quickly, her body lurched with a downward pull. They were descending, deeper into the stone lair she was trapped inside.

A moment, a millisecond, or maybe a minute later, every molecule within her leapt forward and slammed into the front of her body, threatening to fly free. He stopped abruptly, releasing her to settle on wobbly legs.

Dana struggled for balance while the momentum from their travel was still in play. She danced across the floor for a few seconds before coming to a stop and assuming a defensive posture.

He stood, feet away, staring at her. It was the monster who'd killed her mother. He was who the darkness had hidden so well and likely the reason he'd chosen to keep himself shielded from her earlier.

She dredged up the painful memories, recalling how he'd shielded himself the night of her mother's murder. She'd caught a quick glimpse of him when he ran towards her for the split second he'd used to check on his injured man.

"He was my brother," his raspy voice declared, a voice she would never forget.

The sound inside this room bounced back at her like it had nowhere else to go but be absorbed into their bodies. Aside from her mother's screams, his was the only voice she remembered from that horrific night.

Dana's mind burst into an explosion of thoughts. Could he read her mind? Her instinct to kill him made her body quake, but she fought the intense ache so she could collect her bearings. She couldn't stop her hand from trembling, nor would rage let go of the strong hold it had on her.

On second thought, being in such close proximity, she wasn't sure she had the presence of mind to stay in place. He was stronger and faster, she knew as much; therefore, she would have to use strategy if she was to take his head or heart. She glanced at her hand, still bloody from snatching and cradling a heart.

"The one you killed when you were a little girl, he was my brother and one of my only weaknesses. He is the reason you know the sound of my voice."

He's reading my mind.

Dana scanned the room, attempting to plot an escape route, but it appeared they were in a room-sized tomb. The sparse lighting from one low flickering sconce high on the stone wall only let her see a few feet past his shadowy figure. Thankfully, her eyes were starting to adjust, allowing her a view of his ghostly face.

"There's one way out of this room, and I'm the only one who knows it. I didn't bring you here to kill you."

Dana talked through gritted teeth, struggling to stop herself from doing something stupid. "We're locked in a tomb?" she spat. "What do you want if you don't want to kill me? My impulse to kill you is consuming me as I speak. The longer I'm in here with you, the less likely I'll hold myself in place. You're going to have to kill me or let me go."

His cheeks rose in what must have been his attempt at a smile. "You're one of the strongest I've seen in a long time. I've never seen a huntress exhibit this much control. It is said that your impulse to kill us is three times stronger than our thirst for blood, which means you have better control than you're giving yourself credit for. Also, I've never seen one of you take a heart either."

He chuckled like his words weren't confusing the fuck out of her. "I don't often find myself surprised, but it astounded me that you and your boyfriend broke through a witch's spell and used your abilities. It's not often I'm left this intrigued, Dana."

She was sure he hadn't missed her slack-jawed expression. He spoke of witches, abilities, and expelled hearts like it was normal. She worked among agents with abilities, but everyone was so tightlipped about it that it wasn't often brought up in public and was still a forbidden subject even among the gifted. However, just as Neal had never been exposed to these types of creatures, she supposed she'd never considered that witches existed.

A huntress? Is that what I am?

"Come now, Dana. There are people like me and you roaming this planet, and you're having a difficult time processing witches? I had a witch cast a spell on this house against all abilities, except for those of us who live here. You and your boyfriend found a loophole. And yes, you're a huntress."

What was he talking about? How could she and Neal know anything about breaking a witch's spell?

"There is only one force strong enough to break a witch's spell. It is also the one force strong enough to heal almost anything."

"What?" her mind screamed.

"Love."

The word hung in the air like a runaway musical note. Dana's lips fell apart at the revelation. She was fully aware of her feelings for Neal, but it was astonishing that they shared a bond strong enough to fight forces she didn't yet understand.

The images of witches in her head evaporated as quickly as

they entered it. The deep-seated urges she fought in the presence of this monster returned with a vengeance. It was an all-consuming ache she didn't know how to control. All she wanted to do was rip his head off, torture him, and roast his decapitated head over an open flame for at least a week.

Since you're intent upon reading my mind, did you get the part about how badly I want to kill you? She glared at him with a condescending smirk, sensing him eavesdropping on her thoughts.

He cupped his hands in front of him, ignoring the deadly message she'd sent. "I didn't kill your mother. You were a child. There was no way you could have understood what you were seeing."

Dana remained in place, taking deep and deliberate breaths. The more his voice bounced off the walls, the more she wanted to kill him. Her fists were clenched so tightly, the pinch of her nails digging into her flesh was a relief.

"I saw when you killed my mother. You bit her. You and your men drank her blood. You snapped her neck."

She clutched her hands behind her back to steady them.

"What you saw was a part of a ceremony my family performs when one of us crosses over. I didn't kill your mother. None of us killed your mother. We merely took a part of her into ourselves, and, in return, she was given a part of us."

A minute part of her will to kill him slipped away at his demented words. Was he mentally unstable? Nothing he said held logic and trying to make sense of it only added fuel to her irritation.

He took a step closer, and she couldn't figure out if he was being bold or giving her a reason to fight him.

"I didn't bring you in here to fight you. I didn't kill your mother, either."

"What the hell are you saying? Make me understand. Otherwise, we *will* be fighting."

Her jaw ticked hard, and her right eye twitched from the amount of burning rage racing through her veins and flooding her mind with images of death. His death.

She pointed a stiff finger at him. "You're not going to play your mind tricks on me. I know that some of you know some kind of voodoo. You and your kind killed my mother. I saw it with my own eyes. The one who bit me died. I don't know why he died, but I've been searching all this time to make sure the rest of you die too."

He lifted a hand in the universal sign signaling her to stop. Could he sense that she was on the verge of saying, *"Fuck the conversation and let's fight until one of us dies?"*

"Dana, you have been killing your own family members. The one who bit you was my brother. He was your great-great uncle, Lazlo."

A burst of sarcastic laughter flew past her lips. This man was crazier than a pigeon after it accidently ate crack.

"I'm not crazy, and I can assure you that every word I'm speaking is the truth. Lazlo was the weakest among us, so I'm sure he couldn't resist the scent of your blood. Your blood is what killed him. The blood of a virgin huntress is toxic to us. It also smells so incredibly good it's nearly impossible to resist."

"Deep breaths," she coached herself. None of this shit was true.

"Age makes us stronger, but not even age could have saved Lazlo. He'd always been a slave to blood. Although it wasn't your intent to kill him, his death triggered your ability. After your first kill, you should have developed an irresistible need to seek out and kill our kind. All vampires."

Holy hell.

Her head dropped at his confirmation. She'd been lying to herself for years, attempting to convince herself that those weren't vampires who'd killed her mother.

"Once a hunter or huntress makes his or her first vampire

kill, intentional or accidental, it triggers your ability. The trigger also feeds into your insatiable desire to kill us. You're a huntress. It's embedded in your DNA to rid this world of us, and you can't control it or turn it off any more than I can control being a vampire or my need for blood."

She shook her head, brushing away his statement. She didn't want to hear any more of this madness, but his voice kept coming, an irritating nuisance ripping apart the darkness.

"I understand you better than you can imagine. I know that your need to kill us is stronger than our thirst for blood, yet we share the same bloodline."

He took a breath.

Why? It wasn't like he needed air to stay alive.

"In case you haven't figured it out yet, I'm your great-great grandfather. I would have put a stop to this sooner if we could have identified that it was you coming after our men. You kept up your perfect daughter routine so well, we never suspected you were the one coming after us all these years."

His words made her knees go weak. Dana couldn't move. She had the sinking feeling he was telling the truth, but she couldn't accept it. She was not going to accept it.

"There is no way in hell I'm kin to you. You're lying, you murdering bastard. You killed my mother, and you're spreading lies and using trickery to justify it."

Tears filled Dana's eyes. Her unbearable anger wouldn't let up. As soon as Linkin dropped his gaze, Sevyn stared back at him. Totally out of control, it did feel like she truly was two different people because Sevyn didn't give a fuck about dying.

She pounced on him, using her speed to attack.

Linkin straight-armed her so quickly, she hardly had time to react. He yanked her back as fast as she had charged at him. She spun away from his tight hold and sent an elbow up to his face, but he ducked in time. Her leg shot up, her knee rushing towards his midsection, but the bastard was faster.

She retrieved the knife she had snatched from the heartless one downstairs and kept in her waistband. When it plunged into his chest, he didn't even flinch. He simply yanked the knife out and tossed it aside like it was an unwanted toothpick. The metal clinked against the stone floor and echoed off the walls.

Does he even have a heart?

CHAPTER TWENTY-SIX

DANA

"Dana, stop it, baby. Please!"

The female voice stopped her dead in her tracks. When the familiar sound stroked her eardrums, she immediately recognized it.

It couldn't be. She had watched her die. She had seen them all bite away pieces of her flesh. They drank her blood. She'd watched her neck get snapped. She'd sat through her funeral and had kissed her cold cheek as she lay in a flower-shrouded coffin. She'd stood there and watched her be lowered into a grave before she placed extra, twice-kissed, white roses atop the coffin.

Dana's eyes slid closed, and she turned on noodled legs. She'd never been a fainter, but in this moment, her legs threatened to buckle. There, standing feet in front of her, was her mother.

She slammed her eyes shut and shook her head to ward off the haunting image, but the vision refused to go away. This was a mind trick Linkin was playing on her. He could manipulate darkness; surely, he could manifest a copy of her mother.

"It's me, Dinky."

The sound of the voice made Dana jump. A tear slid down her cheek, and her lips trembled in a mix of emotion and anger. Her mother was the only one who called her Dinky. Not even her father knew of her secret nickname.

Even if this was a trick, seeing a full image of her mother again, made her heart swell.

"How? I watched you die. They killed you. We had your funeral."

She was paler, her once light caramel skin almost white, but there was no mistaking her mother's beautiful features. The long curly hair, her perfectly symmetrical face, and her always smiling eyes.

Dana believed her mother was the most beautiful woman in the world. Each time someone complimented her mother, Dana felt proud.

Growing up, she'd been told by her family and friends that she was a darker, spitting image of her mother. What better compliment was there than to look like the most beautiful woman in the world?

Her mother had always been nice and loving, the kind of person everyone fell in love with. Her death had torn Dana apart. It took years for her to rebuild her mind and allow her broken heart to mend. Her wounds had scabbed, but she'd never fully healed and feared she never would until she caught and killed all the monsters responsible for her mother's death.

She swiped at her wet eyes, unable to accept what was in front of her.

"I'm so sorry. I wish I could have found a way to explain this to you, before now." The image took a deep breath before continuing. "Linkin revealed the truth to you. They weren't trying to kill me that night. The truth was that I was becoming too dangerous to be around you. I didn't trust myself around my own baby girl anymore. I was such a danger to you I had no choice but to cross over and stay away from you."

The woman reached out, but Dana stumbled back.

"Even if I believe any of the shit you two are feeding me, how are you still alive? Have you become one of them? Were you one of them the entire time?"

The longer she stood there, the more she sensed this woman was truly her mother. The woman lifted pleading hands, and she could see the tremble in them in the dim lighting.

"I didn't have a choice. In this family, you have two options. You get the hunters gene, like you have, or you get the vampire gene, like I have. Few people know that hunters are direct descendants of vampires."

Dana stood slack-jawed. *What the fuck was she saying?* It sounded an awful lot like she was insinuating she'd descended from monsters. Could any of this shit actually be true?

"I spent years chasing monsters to avenge your death, and you're saying that you're one of them? Have been one of them all along? You've been alive this entire time and let me believe you were dead?"

She pleaded, "Dinky, please remain calm so I can explain this to you?"

She reached for her arm, and Dana jerked away.

"No, I will not remain calm while you're standing there telling me that I'm a monster. But, I don't have much choice in listening to you since my *great-great-grandfather* over there is the only one who knows the way out of here."

Dana glanced back and noticed Linkin hadn't moved an inch since her supposed mother started talking. The woman ushered a hand towards the man.

"This truly is your great-great grandfather, Linkin Morvant. When one is born with true vampire blood, three things will happen. One, you immediately become a vampire and grow into maturity at a rapid pace. Two, your vampirism lies dormant and may, or may not, manifest. In my case, it decided to manifest itself when I was well into adulthood. I have no idea what triggered it but being around you was too dangerous.

"When I started craving human flesh, I knew something was wrong. The day I almost bit you was the last straw. I had to figure out what was wrong with me. I had cravings I couldn't control. I went to every doctor I could find and none of them could tell me what was wrong with me.

"Linkin sensed my call because I was transitioning. Our bloodline connection was how he knew I was out there. I had no idea I was linked to a family of vampires because I didn't even know what I was. I had no idea vampires even existed."

Dana's body swayed from the impact of the revelations bombarding her mind. This whole time, she'd assumed she was the good guy, helping humanity and saving the world from monsters, when she was a spawn of the very things she was hunting. All she could think now was, *Am I the Hero or the Villain?*

"Traditional vampire families like the Vandracks and Nikolaevichs, before even your great-great-grandfather's time, would cast out those like you or me. We, the Morvants, followed the traditions. Therefore, those like me and you were deserted and labeled as *hindered* because we were underdeveloped by vampire standards.

"They considered it a serious disability if you didn't immediately turn. Back then, many members were banished from their families and, in some cases, abandoned to fend for themselves. Those were the members of our species who later developed into vampires without having a full understanding of their nature. Those were the ones who usually ran wild, killing with no mercy, or rules to follow."

Dana's fingers closed, pinching the bridge of her nose. She glanced up, wide-eyed, from underneath her hand at the woman. She still hadn't fully extinguished the idea that she'd been trapped in some type of mind trick.

"Those who inherit the hunter's gene evolved into a species that didn't need family for survival or strength. They developed such a strong hatred for our kind that they were blinded by rage and sought revenge on the beings who rejected them. The hatred evolved into a force so powerful, it sharpens their natural instincts and activates their abilities, the gifts that would have developed had they become vampires. The hunter's gene keeps the family from sensing you like they sensed me. It eats away your thirst for blood and replaces it with a thirst of a different kind. A thirst to shed vampire blood. The original vampire hunters, before the *hindered* came along, were the protectors of our kind and used to hunt down and protect us from our enemies.

"Within the last couple of hundred years, the vampire species has teetered on the verge of extinction and can no longer afford to cast away what they once considered *hindered*. They developed a plan. If we didn't immediately turn upon birth, we were entrusted to a human family who knew our history in case we peaked later."

Dana's brain hurt from this history lesson. Her breaths filled the space, the sound amplified along with her steady foot to foot shifting to keep her raging energy in check.

"The humans who raised me were killed when I was fourteen, so there was no one to tell me, or to explain to me, what I was, or what I might go through when, and if, the time came. I was a *toddler*, meaning I had no idea I possessed a supernatural ability or that I was other than human. By the time I got the call from Linkin to meet him, I was so desperate to figure out what was wrong I ran to him, begging for help."

At this point, Dana recalled a few of those incidences. Her mother was acting funny, snapping at her, and becoming easily upset. She remembered going with her to meet with someone, but it was always inside the hospital, so she naturally assumed her mother was seeing a doctor.

"Things had gotten so bad that your father was thinking of having me committed. I kept myself hidden and away from you as much as possible by pawning you off on the nannies and locking myself in one of the guest bedrooms. One night, I locked myself in the basement.

"At first, I didn't believe Linkin about our history and what I was, but I was desperate enough to continue meeting with him. You weren't safe being alone with me anymore. I was turning, and I couldn't control myself."

Dana clung to every word, although she continued to struggle with her raging urge to kill.

"By the time the family reached me, I was so far gone they didn't have a choice but to start the crossover ceremony. They each had to take a part of me into their bodies—blood and flesh. I was losing my mind, so I fought them when all they were trying to do was help me. You heard my screams that night and assumed they were hurting me."

The crease Dana felt between her eyes deepened. *Could this shit be true?*

"A drop of blood from an immediate family member eases the turn, makes the process less hostile. I was losing control, so they had a difficult time keeping me calm. You ran into my bedroom and, as little as you were, you tried to help me without concern for your own life. Your Uncle Lazlo had to restrain you, so he held you down. Things went wrong when he bit you on the arm."

Dana instinctively rubbed the spot where he'd left a scar on the inside of her right wrist.

"The scent of your blood is what caused him to lose his composure. I wasn't fully turned, and it was hard for me to resist the scent of it. When your uncle bit you and died, it sent everyone in the room into a panic. No one knew what it meant, so they broke my neck to shut me up, knowing it wouldn't kill me. They locked you in the closet and took me to finish the ceremony. After they coached me on how to fake my death, I returned home and did as they instructed until I was put into the ground.

"I..." her voice cracked and glistening tears bounced off the sparse lighting and slipped down her cheeks. "I was the one who believed it was best to stay away from you. It wasn't until after I'd turned that I found out that you would someday turn too, so I kept an eye on you from afar. It wasn't until you took Drago a few weeks ago that we discovered it was you who had been hunting us the entire time."

This was too damn much to process. She was a second from asking them to produce a damn book and mail it to her so she could unburden herself this ache of burning rage suffocating her.

"It took us years to figure out what exactly killed Lazlo as no one had ever encountered or considered that a virgin huntress' blood was lethal to vampires. No one had any idea what you were or that your uncle's bite had triggered you that night. We had no history telling us that a mother could carry the vampire gene while her daughter could carry the hunters. The incident that night, after we had pieced it all together, made you the youngest huntress we knew of in our history, at ten years old."

She swiped at a tear with the back of her hand, her sorrowful gaze locked on Dana.

"You see, Dinky, I couldn't reunite with you if I wanted to. You'd have the urge to kill me. When we discovered who you were a few weeks ago, and that you were hunting who you believed killed me, I begged the family to allow me to tell you the truth about us. But it is extremely difficult for hunters and vampires to share the same space without wanting to rip each other apart."

Dana shuffled faster, rocking from foot to foot and forcing the weight of her urges to shift with her body.

"Vampires are so few now that we fear becoming extinct and

have started seeking out our kind. Very few of us have the ability to reproduce, and those who can are producing only *hindered* children. Despite legends and myths, we can't turn whoever we want. We reproduce like any other species. There were a few of us who had the gift to turn anyone, but they died out hundreds of years ago. The family could have helped me turn sooner had they known how to find me, but I'm glad they didn't because I wouldn't have had the chance to have you."

Dana soaked it all in, and although her mother's sobs tore at her heart, she wouldn't or couldn't relent. Should she believe this inconceivable story or follow her raging instincts that insisted she kill these monsters? The ache to kill was like a repeating mantra screaming in her head and pulsing in her blood, so loud her body trembled to contain it.

"If I understand you clearly, I'm a descendant of vampires. I have vampire blood coursing through my veins and by some glorious miracle, I hate vampires. Let's see, one of three things were bound to happen. One, after birth, I'd immediately become a vampire, where I would have killed myself the first chance I got. Two, my vampirism would remain dormant and surfaced at some point, where I would have killed myself the first chance I got. Or three, I would go completely rogue, let my rage for being forsaken take control, and seek out and kill the very thing I was born from."

Her mother threw up her hands, pleading for her under-standing. If what they were saying was true, then they should have understood that closing her off in a room with them was not a good idea. There was only but so much control she could exert over something built into her DNA.

"Dinky, I know this is a lot to swallow, but it is all true."

Dana had no doubt her mother's slumped posture and deeply creased face was an extension of her broken heart. However, she wasn't ready to accept any of these new developments.

She tightened her already folded arms across her chest, allowing the tight squeeze to absorb some of the body-quaking tension racing through her. "If this is all true, we have nothing further to talk about. All I ask is that you never reveal yourself to my father. Your death ripped him apart, and I don't want him hurting all over again."

Why was she shaking her head, knowing what Dana was fighting to keep herself from doing at the moment?

"I'll never stop wanting to kill you, and you'll never stop thirsting for my blood. There is nothing more we need to say to each other. There is nothing more we could ever do for each other except stay away."

As hard as it was for Dana to turn away from the woman she loved unconditionally, she found the strength to force her body to move. As hard as it was for her to accept, her urge to kill her own mother was so strong, she would have done it if she didn't think Linkin would stop her. She turned to face him with caution, her aching body demanding she unleash the pent-up rage threatening to drive her mad.

"Are you going to let me out or what?"

He didn't reply.

Her mother was immediately in front of her with tears streaming down her cheeks. "I love you. Always have. Always will."

Dana didn't respond. As hard as it was to suppress her urges, it didn't stop her heart from filling with love for her mother. She zipped around her and ran with lightning-fast speed, knowing her great-great-grandfather was fast enough to stop her before she followed her natural-born instincts to kill them.

She didn't know if it took seconds or milliseconds for him to snatch her up again, but he returned her to the main lobby of the lair. Now, she fully understood her strong compulsion to kill them was something she couldn't have helped no matter what.

The one whose heart she'd taken was a puddle of blood on the floor. The realization pleased her. It was confirmation she'd discovered another way to kill them. She found Neal leaning against the wall where she'd been torn from his grip. Upon seeing her, he straightened his posture and exuded strength, but failed to conceal the concern in his hiked brows and creased forehead.

"I'm fine. Let's get out of here, before I stop fighting my impulses and end up getting us killed."

No one moved to stop her when she and Neal marched towards what she hoped was the front door.

CHAPTER TWENTY-SEVEN

DANA

AFTER ALL THE truth she had discovered, Dana needed time to process it. Since her office was under construction, she had a break from her day job. She also found the strength to call a truce with her newly discovered family. The only one she'd not promised to go after was Drago since he was on TOP's kill list.

She had a strange sense her mother, or perhaps any one of her new family members, were continuing to keep tabs on her. She'd accidently killed one of them when she was a little girl, hunted down and murdered two more, and had likely permanently disfigured another.

If their family history was true, Dana would find a way to keep killing them, and there wasn't a thing she could do about it except fight to control the kill gene she inherited. Her heart longed for her mother, and she wasn't altogether sure she could stop herself from meeting with her if the opportunity presented itself. However, she had to find a way to accept that her mother died when she was ten or risk opening a whole new can of worms.

She could picture herself becoming a stalker of TOP's supernatural history library, attempting to find information that could substantiate the past her mother and Linkin had laid out.

She also planned to retake the supernatural history courses TOP offered and was now starting to understand why other agents retook them. You didn't really take the courses seriously until you were met with that one assignment, or revelation, that changed your life.

Although she found the story of her history hard to swallow, she couldn't think of anything else that would explain her abilities. Now, she needed to find a way to live with the cold hard truth, not only of her history, but of her blood.

Hours later and after Dana had gotten cleaned up and her mind had somewhat settled, she smiled for the first time since leaving that lair. There was one thing that could help alleviate her suffering and ease her mind of monsters, and he stood before her, undressing her with his eyes.

Neal was the glue that kept her mind intact. And although she knew the agency would eventually call for him, she planned to make whatever time they had left count.

They stood apart for a few moments more, admiring each other, her smile enticing his to surface. She strutted over to him, unable to fight the urgent need he had the power to build within her. Standing on tiptoe, she allowed her lips to graze his ear.

"You intoxicate me. Do you know that?"

He didn't respond, but those eyes conveyed enough lust to melt her clothes off her body. At times, like now, it appeared he held doubts about how desirable she found him. Despite his lingering bouts of doubt, it didn't take them long to become so enraptured in each other that they forgot about everything else in the world.

Hours later, when the dust settled and nerves had calmed, Dana divulged everything to Neal. She told him about her heritage, about her mother, and about Linkin.

Neal took the news with ease and never cast one judgmental eye on her. His acceptance of her, spliced vampire gene and all, let her know that he was unquestionably the man for her.

CHAPTER TWENTY-EIGHT

DANA

THE AUGUST HEAT HAD PEOPLE, human and others, doing crazy things. The news headlines were an explosion of strange and violent acts. For once, Dana stayed away from it all. She'd decided to take a break from chasing crazy.

Although she'd been determined to stay away from her mother, she couldn't help answering her phone when she received a call from her every other week. There were never any words, only the open line between them for one minute.

She hadn't seen Neal in months. With TOP, every assignment was an urgent one and, as she had expected, an urgent operation had torn Neal away from her. Her thoughts of him kept her company despite the mountain of financial documents surrounding her.

Work *somewhat* kept her mind occupied. The scent of new paint still permeated the suite. It had taken nearly two months to complete her office renovations, and she'd taken advantage by adding a few upgrades.

She'd had a custom-made desk built as well as a secret compartment added to her office closet. The arsenal of guns and knives she kept in both areas were enough to start a war.

Her ten employees resumed their normal routines after their scare. A pay raise, as well as the opportunity to attend therapy sessions on the company dime, helped to boost morale.

Jordan cracked her door open and peeked inside. "There's someone here to see you."

She didn't like to accept uninvited guests. Since she wasn't expecting Neal for another week, she prayed it wasn't one of her bad romances trying to reconnect.

"Are they on the calendar? I didn't think I had anyone coming in today."

"I need to be on the calendar to see you now?"

Neal shoved the door open, and the smile on Dana's face grew into a wide affectionate grin. Jordan gave her a head nod and walked away with a huge smile as well.

She ran to Neal, tackling him with a strong hug. His kisses melted her before his warm lips peppered her face with sweet strokes of love and passion she soaked up like a sponge.

"I missed you so much," she blurted.

She squeezed him hard enough to make him release a strangled cough. Her arms loosened before she unhooked them, stepped back, and allowed her gaze to meet his. Her prolonged stare put a touch of tension in his forehead.

"Wow, you *did* miss me?" he questioned, appearing stunned by the emotions he must have spotted reflected in her expression.

"Yes. I missed you more than I miss burning heads."

They maintained another prolonged stare while his fingers skimmed delicately over her cheek.

"That's a whole lot of missing me."

He had no idea how deeply he'd reached into her heart, and her determination to show him was scratching at her surface. His soft kisses landed on her lips, her cheeks, her neck, and left a heated desire that jumpstarted her already heightened emotions. He not only had her gaze pinned, but her mind was fully engaged. She was unable to look anywhere except into his eyes while he positioned her face in a delicate caress between his palms.

"Dana, the kind of life we live has given no promises that either of us will see tomorrow. These last few assignments have given me a new perspective on life. TOP is expanding my agent portfolio where it concerns the types of cases they are assigning me now. I want to spend time with you, whenever it's available."

She nodded, and the depth of concern he fought to keep off his face let her know that his recent assignment must have been hell.

"Of course. Me too."

His forehead wrinkled, and care and concern flashed in the depth of his searching gaze. "Dana, I love you. I can't go another day without you knowing how I truly feel."

Touched, she didn't stop the tears that pooled and threatened to fall from her unblinking eyes. She kissed him, her lips crashing into his in an emotional rush.

"I love you too," she murmured, smashing the endearing words into his lips. She palmed his face and neck after three tries of easing out of their kiss. "I'm in love with you, Neal, so much so that I can confidently say I don't want any other man kissing me, holding me, or making love to me. You're the only one that I'll allow to devour me."

He flashed a big grin before they fell back into each other's arms. The abundance of flowing emotions had them vying to show the other how much they truly loved the other.

The caring kisses dissolved into steamy, passion-laden caresses, gropes, and grabs. The unstoppable passion ignited their senses and took possession of their minds, causing their labored breaths to mingle into one desperate sound that filled her office with remnants of their affections.

"Let's go, before my employees hear me lose control of myself. It's bad enough you have me in here confessing my undying love for you. I can literally gag on all of this cheesy emotion we're spilling."

He laughed at her rapid-fire movements as she shut down her computer and threw files into her desk drawer. The tip of her French-tipped nail pushed a red blinking button and a beep sounded before she began speaking into her desk phone.

"Jordan, I'm taking the rest of the day off. Unless it's a matter of life and limb, it can wait until Monday."

Work be damned, she had more important things to do, and he was about six-two and sexy as hell.

She grabbed her purse. "I have an entire weekend to show you how much I missed you. I don't want to be quiet about it, so were checking into a hotel."

Dana and Neal ended up checking in to the luxurious Sparks Hotel a few blocks from her office. She walked in and scanned the room with fast roving eyes. After throwing her key card and purse on the table, she took Neal's hand and dragged him towards the marble steps leading to a huge, elevated four-poster bed.

The room exuded sophistication, but neither noticed. They only had eyes for each other.

Neal stopped Dana from climbing into bed with a strong hand around her waist. His fingers explored before they turned the golden knobs of her buttons, pulling them free of the small slices of material that kept them in place. Freeing her from her navy pantsuit, her sexy, red-laced bra revealed itself with each turn of his fingers. His hot pink tongue circled his sexy lips with purpose.

"What do you want me to do to you?"

She loved that he asked. Whenever she made her suggestions, he acted accordingly in fulfilling her request. Her anxious hands ended up in the waistband of his jeans. A tug lured him closer and allowed her to inhale his heady scent. Her lips raked his ear before she released her seductive whisper.

"I want you to take these clothes off me, but in a way that excites my senses."

The magnetic pull he had on her libido enticed her to tease her tongue along his lobe. His shirt was lifted, pulled over his head, and tossed while the fluidity of her words continued.

"Tease me as you disrobe me, and I want you to use your fingers to make me dripping wet." She paused to nip at his chin playfully. "Then, I want you to lay me right there on the end of that bed and spread my legs."

Her body leaned into his, flowing into the movements of the erotic storm they produced together. A teasing pinch trapped his lobe between her fingers, and she tugged him down by the ear to her waiting mouth.

She nibbled playfully before sending more seductive words into his ears. "I would like to be in the throes of my first orgasm by the time I'm completely naked." She eased his zipper down before taking a firm grip of his pants, still mouthing off instructions of what she wanted done to her.

He lifted and toed each of his feet from his boots before working his legs from his pants and kicking them aside.

She stood and wiggled her finger for him to come closer so she could finish whispering the rest of her dirty little fantasy in his ear. He jerked his head back, and she enjoyed seeing his wide-eyed reaction at her hot request.

"Is that right? A threesome. You, me, and Sevyn?"

Neal rubbed his hands together, like he was about to enjoy a feast fit for a king.

Dana threw a finger up, to emphasize another statement. "If you have energy after that, I want you to make slow, passionate love to me, and show me how much you love me with the motion of your strokes."

He kissed along her chin and neck and lower, placing tender pecks to her shoulders, down her chest to her stomach, and thighs while freeing her from the rest of her clothes.

"I'll be happy to put an end to your suffering," he replied.

Damn.

She loved this man. Dana had no idea if Neal could accomplish *all* the sexual favors she'd asked for, but he would do his best to make it happen. The idea had her sexual energy vibrating at the prospect of him giving her the satisfaction she knew he could deliver.

EPILOGUE

NEAL CAME awake with a hard jolt. He sat up with a hand at his throat from choking on the big intakes of oxygen he was sucking in, his body heaving and his eyes wide. The warmth of Dana's hand running along his back and arm was what pulled him completely out of his mixed-up state of panic and mind-bending awareness.

Only after she'd coaxed him with calm hands back to a normal breathing pattern did she ask, "Bad dream? Are you okay?"

He nodded. His mouth was so dry he sent his tongue on a search mission for moisture. A hard swallow followed, and he still hadn't managed to open his eyes. Every drop of his strength had been poured into what he had experienced while sleeping. A deep inhale and a slow exhale allowed him to open his eyes and turn his head just enough to look into Dana's eyes.

"The nineteen years missing from my memory." His words rushed out in a blur of breathless sounds. "I remember what happened to me."

"What? What happened to you? Where were you?" Dana's words pushed out just as quickly as his rushed ones.

"It's real. It's a real place. And I've been there," he whispered before his stressed glare pushed deeper into Dana's wide one.

"I was kidnapped by a priest who kept me as his prisoner in *the Hollow*."

FREE BOOK ALERT!!!!!

NEAL – A PARANORMAL NOVELLA

Nineteen missing years and a wicked scar. Sounds like an interesting concept to me. If you enjoyed Sevyn and are interested in learning more about Neal, his novella is available now!

All you have to do to receive an early and free download of this novella is sign up for Keta Kendric's Paranormal newsletter.

https://mailchi.mp/38b87cb6232d/keta-kendric-paranormal-newsletter

AUTHOR'S NOTE

Readers, my sincere thank you for reading Sevyn. Although I've become known for mafia and motorcycle club romances, paranormal romance is where I started my writing journey. Therefore, I had to pay literary respects to my writing roots. Please leave a review letting me and others know what you thought of Sevyn. If you enjoyed it or any of my other books, please pass them along to friends or anyone you think would enjoy them.

OTHER TITLES BY KETA KENDRIC

CONNECT ON SOCIAL MEDIA

Subscribe to my Paranormal Newsletter for exclusive updates on new releases, sneak peeks, and much more.

You can also follow me on:

Instagram: instagram.com/ketakendric
Facebook Readers' Group:
facebook.com/groups/380642765697205/
BookBub: bookbub.com/authors/keta-kendric
Twitter: twitter.com/AuthorKetaK
Goodreads: goodreads.com/user/show/73387641-keta-kendric
TikTok: tiktok.com/@ketakendric?
Newsletter Sign up: https://mailchi.mp/38b87cb6232d/keta-kendric-paranormal-newsletter

Made in the USA
Middletown, DE
22 March 2024